Allen Samuel

The Demon of the Orient, and His Satellite Fiends of the Joints. Our Opium Smokers as They are in Tartar Hells and American Paradises

Allen Samuel Williams

The Demon of the Orient, and His Satellite Fiends of the Joints. Our Opium Smokers as They are in Tartar Hells and American Paradises

Reprint of the original, first published in 1883.

1st Edition 2024 | ISBN: 978-3-38533-236-2

Verlag (Publisher): Outlook Verlag GmbH, Zeilweg 44, 60439 Frankfurt, Deutschland
Vertretungsberechtigt (Authorized to represent): E. Roepke, Zeilweg 44, 60439 Frankfurt, Deutschland
Druck (Print): Books on Demand GmbH, In de Tarpen 42, 22848 Norderstedt, Deutschland

THE

DEMON OF THE ORIENT

AND HIS

Satellite Fiends of the Joints:

OUR OPIUM SMOKERS AS THEY ARE IN
TARTAR HELLS AND AMERICAN
PARADISES.

BY ALLEN S. WILLIAMS.

New York:
PUBLISHED BY THE AUTHOR.

for they had no guard on their outer edges. Sing seemed to have so much confidence in "Frank," my companion, and to be so well acquainted with him, that he left him to make himself at home, and myself as well, so that we wandered about as curiosity or inclination moved us.

We paused a moment in the second room, where four Chinaman were playing "fan-tan." This—their favorite gambling pursuit, next to lottery—is a crude invention. A pile of glittering pieces of metal, either cone, wedge, or disk shaped, is covered by an inverted bowl. The bowl is lifted off and the "dealer" cuts the pile into four parts, scraping away three. The players then bet on the number of pieces in the remaining pile, and the player, who comes the nearest in his estimate, "rakes the pot." This then is *tan* as near as an inquisitive American can make it out. The nearest approach to it that we possess is, perhaps, the "hog guessings" in some remote rural districts organized in the Winter holidays for sport and profit. *Tan* and its rules are not described by Hoyle; and its accompaniment of profanity in Pigeon English, and invocation of demoniac powers in Chinese would necessitate by their inclusion an enlargement of his invaluable *vade mecum* for gamesters.

To the rear was a small room apparently dedicated to religion and tea drinking. Against a wooden partition stood a bureau divested of the crowning glory of its cheap toilet mirror, but transformed with mats, and *kakemonos* or scrolls, and drapery into an altar, while above it hung a china censer. Upon the altar were various heathen mysteries in lacquer, wicker, silk, and china—good specimens of decorative art—also little pots, paints, and brushes, while Joss sticks, resembling the punk used by Young America to light his fire crackers on the "glorious Fourth," aromatically smouldered in toy candle sticks. Beside the altar stood a tall china jar of undrawn tea ; above it, over a lamp-stove, hung an earthenware tea-kettle with a wicker handle. The flame burned steadily just high enough to keep the kettle hot. "Now do stay to tea; it's all

ready," said my companion, in a mock tone of feminine
entreaty, as he unceremoniously reached for two fragile
translucent cups upon the altar, which served conve-
niently for a side board. We drank the beverage, which
he poured from the kettle, straight. Without a desire
to puff one branch of the tea trade at the expense of
the other I may remark that all the tea I have drank
in Chinatown was delicious. Perhaps "Ah Sin," with
all his accredited duplicity, is unequal to the deleterious
shams and tricks and cheats of the American tea trade
in its stages from *some* of the Water street importers,
jobbers, and mixers, to the gaudy stores that inflict
upon the purchaser molded glassware and cheap
chromos with every dollar's worth.

When we re-entered the first room, the regular customers seemed to have all been gathered within the
fold, and business to be progressing satisfactorily, for
Sing was laid up on the shelf, his form curled in a
negligent crescent shape. Sing was doing his own
cooking, and as he lay with his face close to the small
lamp he used—there was but one general coal-oil lamp,
with a dirty chimney, to illuminate the whole room—
his countenance seem sicklied o'er with a pale cast of
poisonous contentment.

"Was George here, to-night, Sing ?" asked the white
fiend of the yellow.

The latter had compressed his lips upon the big bamboo stem of the pipe, however, and was steadily drawing in the smoke. This inhalation being succeeded by
a series of disjointed sucks. The opium boiled and
sizzled, and the fragrant smoke floated upward. The
sybarite and slave rubbed all the opium up to the small
orifice in the bowl, so as not to lose any of the precious
poppy juice, and then slowly taking the pipe from his
mouth, replied :

"No."

"Well, was he here last night ?"

"No, Flank; Jlorge him not bleen here tlee nights,"
answered Sing, in his pigeon English.

Up to the time of this writing the husband has entirely abstained from drink, but was unable to resist the attraction of his old associates of the joints, and returned to his old companions and shortly afterwards resumed the *yen tsiang.*

The wife, whose cure has been a veritable elixir of youth, and who could scarcely be recognized by any who had seen her a year ago, was still devoted enough to her worthless husband to accompany him back to the joints, where she cooks for him, but has never yet been seen to smoke herself. If her resolution holds out, or if the desire has indeed disappeared, and forever, this will truly prove a marvelous and encouraging case.

A woman who is as well known to the fiends in New York as even Viola Hardinge, is Delia Maguire, or "Barney's girl." If the first mentioned character is entitled to her royal sobriquet, Barney Maguire should at least, be termed the "Prince of the Joints," because of his lavish hospitality. When Barney enters a joint, he is very apt to consider that he has a proprietary interest while he remains, and all the regular patrons and peripatetic fiends present, are wont to choose their liquor and drink their fill, and to accompany opium with tobacco in whatever form it may best please them, leaving it for Barney to "make good" by his own polite request.

Delia alternates her indulgences in the narcotic, with vinous or alcoholic stimulants, and being a madcap in her soberest moments, becomes alternately, jubilant, "hystericky," and fractious when under the influence. The incidents of Delia's sprees furnish conversational topics for a week after they occur to the motley assemblages of the joints, and her rows with Barney are oftentimes ludicrous. The fact of the happy pair being present in *propria persona* is not considered sufficient cause to taboo the subject, and they themselves discuss smilingly their previous misadventures and misunderstandings with as much relish as any gossip in the company.

in Cleveland, and in Chicago I had no trouble in finding joints and companionable fiends at Jim Horn's,
No. 74 East Van Buren street, and at Wing Lee's, No.
342 State street."

"I should not wonder if there were joints in Syracuse for I have heard it stated that there are over 1,000
white opium eaters and smokers in that town alone."

The fiend continued his interesting relation on the
car which carried them back to their starting place.
Before he left he said with a laugh which some way
jarred upon the reporter, as reckless of any consequences to himself: "I shall never ask you to smoke
again, but if you should ever become a fiend, and do
not find the joints handy you can find a place not a
mile away." "Where is that?" asked the reporter.
"Down next to the cigar store in Woh Hop's. He's
got a good pipe there too, I can recommend it myself,"
and with another low laugh the fiend sauntered along
Fourth street, leaving the reporter more curious to
analyze his thoughts and feelings, than he had been to
observe his fiendish methods.

In Philadelphia the evil has taken root, and it means
to spread. Already the *Press* is reproaching the good
Mayor King for his blindness to the evil doings of the
Chinese in the Quaker City. The principal "joint,"
or at least the one best known, is in the building at No.
801 Sansom street. A laundry sign indicates the
honest labor of the celestials, and serves as a blind for
the more lucrative occupation of joint keeping. As
has been often enough proved on the Pacific slope,
when the Chinese once obtain a foothold in a building
its respectability fast fades away. It was so in this
case; disorderly characters now frequent the rooms above
the joint, and a policy shop and faro bank rapidly followed. The opium joint is darkly secreted n the cellar,
and the passive pleasures of the pipe are varied with
the active ones of investing in lottery. Quong Sing
Lung is the laundry man, and a reporter of the *Philadelphia Press* who invaded the sanctum in the rear where

me, and bid the stultified falsity, with its caps and bells and its empty rattle, begone from my mind. And it did go, so far as the tiresome reiteration of it was concerned, but not by my volition or its own. It was crowded out by an intruder so incalculably more tormenting than itself that I prayed the old torture to return, if it could banish the new. Until the deed was done and my purchase achieved, I had been too intent upon its accomplishment to think of any consequences to myself, other than those I had forestalled by secrecy.

"I had regarded it simply as a philosophical experiment, whose only danger was to be overcome by skillful manipulation. No moral, mental or conscientious view of it ever presented itself to me. My random selection had been made with as much indifference as impartiality. I had thought that upon whomever the choice might fall the subject would be a matter of no more moment to me than those that came under my knife in the operating room. The object in view appeared of suffi cient magnitude to justify the sacrifice of whole hecatombs of lives. How much of this was peculiar to myself, how much the effect of professional training, are questions that can be submitted to no sure arbiter.

"The old English law excluded butchers from the jury box in capital cases, because their calling brutalized them, and rendered them careless of life. There would have been more sense in excluding the fraternity on that ground. I am not an unfeeling man in other respects, but until this fearful lesson I placed a light estimate upon human life, in common with the whole guild. I learned too late that I was mistaken in my preconceptions. After the affair was over, and properly should have been dismissed from my mind, it began to stalk before me at all hours and in all places, like a revengeful apparition, representing itself in aspects I had never seen before. My motive dwindled to a pitiable whim, unworthy the serious consideration of a rational being, while the killing expanded itself to a monstrous crime which no inducement could justify. I experi-

infirmity in his case, it had not revealed itself during our interview. Nothing could be more coherent than his narrative, or more forcible than his reasoning.

These considerations unsettled my original conviction of hallucination, and left me in a state of doubt that was the more tantalizing as I saw no means of dissipating it. The quickness with which he discerned the futility of any effort in that direction was an additional proof of the readiness and clearness of his intellect which helped to dispel the theory of a diseased mind. Whether he was wholly unconnected with the man's death, or whether he had murdered him in the manner asserted, were questions equally indeterminable; the absence of all association in one case, and the profound secrecy observed in the other, would alike baffle investigation.

The result of a night's reflection was the conclusion that my surest course of procedure lay with Waldegrave himself. I would ask him to show me the instrument, the acid, the way in which he had handled them, the route he took upon the streets, the points at which he stopped—in short, every minute circumstance that could have attended the commission of the deed. If he was at a loss upon any of these points, I should feel satisfied that the crime existed only in his imagination. If, on the other hand, he was ready and positive respecting every particular, I saw no alternative to accepting his statement as true.

With this object in view, I went to his residence early in the day. As I mounted the steps I was startled at seeing crape on the door. My errand was useless; Waldegrave had been found dead in his study that morning. The autopsy revealed no cause for his death. I took occasion when no one was present to examine the remains. There was a slight puncture in the skin concealed by the left whisker, which, with the subsequent discovery of a hypodermic syringe on a table close to where the body was found, left no doubt in my mind as to the manner of his death.

PRESS PROPHECIES.

Mail and Express, N. Y.

The recent exposures of the iniquities practiced in the "opium joints" of Chinatown will lend additional interest to a forthcoming book written by Allen S. Williams, a metropolitan journalist, late of the *Times* staff. The work will be entitled "The Demon of the Orient, and his Satellite Fiends of the Joints: Our Opium-smokers as They are in Tartar Hells and American Paradises," and will contain a portrait of the author, etched from life by Valerian Gribayedoff. For two years Mr. Williams has been quietly investigating this phase of vice and may reasonably be supposed to know whereof he writes.

Brooklyn Daily Times.

Mr. Allen S. Williams, of 161 and 163 Franklin Street, New York, has in preparation a little volume which bears the title "The Demon of the Orient," and which is devoted to the discussion—extremely timely just at present—of the opium habit as introduced into American cities by the Chinese. The table of contents is a promising one and Mr. Williams' knowledge of the subject, as well as its natural interest to the public, promise an instructive book.

New York World.

Mr. Allen S. Williams has just completed a work entitled "The Demon of the Orient." The book deals with the habit of opium smoking and the dens where this vice is practiced. The swell joints on Sixth avenue and the common joints on Chatham street are both described. Mr. Williams says there are nearly half a million opium victims in the United States.

New York Truth.

Allen S. Williams, a metropolitan journalist, has in press a volume describing the terrible and rapidly increasing vice of opium smoking, entitled "The Demon of the Orient and his Satellite Fiends of the Joints: Our Opium Smokers as they are i Tartar Hells and American Paradises," with a portrait of the author etched from life by Valerian Gribayedoff. Mr. Williams has been quietly pursuing his investigations of this new social evil for nearly two years, and has written many interesting articles in the newspapers and magazines descriptive of the manners and customs of the victims of the opium pipe and the ethics of the joints.

The Nautical Gazette, N. Y.

"The Demon of the Orient, and his Satellite Fiends of the Joints: Our Opium Smokers as they are in Tartar Hells and American Paradises." By Allen S Williams. Mr. Williams, formerly connected with *Truth* and *New York Times*, has just issued a most interesting work under the above title which has hit a timely topic, and one that is exciting a vast amount of interest at the present moment. In his capacity as a newspaper writer—and a brilliant one at that—he has familiarized himself with his subject by actual observation, and in eleven chapters has unfolded a tale of peculiarly thrilling adventure taken from every-day life. He opens wide the doors of the opium dens, and alike lifts the curtains of American houses where this hellish practice has become deeply rooted, and then asks: "What will we Americans do about it?" The work contains a portrait of the author etched from life by Valerian Gribayedoff. Send for a copy, read it, and then join in the just crusade against opium eating and smoking

Morning Journal, N. Y.

Allen S. Williams, a bright young newspaper reporter of this city, has written a book entitled, "The Demon of the Orient." It is to be published this week. The best view of Chinatown in New York ever given will be found in this book, and the whole story of the opium joints in this city is told therein.

TO HENRY BERGH.

A man who has unyieldingly sustained countless attacks of sarcasm at point of pencil and pen; a servant of the cause of humanity whose fealty has never swerved, and who, if erring, has always erred upon the side of mercy, these pages are respectfully dedicated, by the Author.

"Sopha'd on silk, amid her charm-built towers,
Her meads of asphodel and amaranth bowers;
Where Sleep and Silence guard the soft abodes,
In sullen apathy PAPAVER * nods.
Faint o'er her couch in scintillating streams,
Pass the thin forms of Fancy and of Dreams;
Froze by enchantment on the velvet ground,
Fair youths and beauteous ladies glitter round;
On crystal pedestals they seem to sigh,
Bend the meek knee, and lift the imploring eye.

" And now the Sorceress bares her shrivel'd hand,
And circles thrice in air her ebon wand;
Flush'd with new life descending statues talk,
The pliant marble soften:ng as they walk:
With deeper sobs reviving lovers breathe,
Fair bosoms rise, and soft hearts pant beneath;
With warmer lips relenting damsels speak,
And kindling blushes tinge the Parian cheek;
To viewless lutes aerial voices sing,
And hovering loves are heard on rustling wing.

" She waves her wand again !—fresh horrors seize
Their stiffening limbs, their vital currents freeze;
By each cold nymph her marble lover lies,
And iron slumbers seal their glassy eyes.
So with his dread caduceus Hermes led
From the dark region of the imprison'd dead,
Or drove in silent shoals the lingering train
To Night's dull shore, and PLUTO'S dreary reign."

---

* The botanical name of the Poppy, from which Opium is obtained.

TABLE OF CONTENTS.

PREFACE.

Occult and mysterious influences possess a powerful interest for the imagination of thinking people. Astrology, clairvoyancy, mesmerism and the effect of subtle poisons, such as hashish, and opium in its various forms. Interest in the latter has been enhanced by the description of gorgeous dreams and hallucinations wherein appeared visions of fabulous oriental splendors, and broad views of Wonderland in general, by men of fine brain, nervous temperament, vivid imagination and adepts at word painting. It was therefore with a considerable degree of satisfaction that I accepted the opportunity of investigating as a reporter of a metropolitan newspaper the nature and strength of the bonds that imprisoned the despairing victims of a strangely fascinating and strangely horrible vice. The impressions of fiendish society taken by my mind were, however, unexpectedly serious and ineradicable. Since my *debut*, I have gradually collected the material of which this volume is composed, by far the major portion of it having been obtained through personal experience and observation. I recognized that in the peculiar social character of this form of indulgence in opium existed the reason why opium-smoking will, if not legally crushed out, or stringently restricted, rapidly ensnare Young America, and in a few decades of years contest with the Demon Drink for supremacy. The aim of this work is to depict the social aspect of this novel and dreadful vice in a plain way that may be read by all the people. Therapeutics, I leave to the physicians. My earnest wish is to find, or help find, the preventive which is proverbially valued at a dozen times the worth of the cure.

THE DEMON OF THE ORIENT.

CHAPTER I.

A TRIP TO CHINATOWN

THE lower city seemed deserted. It was eleven o'clock of a Tuesday night and the writer hesitated for a moment, under the stone porch of the New York Post Office, while debating whether or not to take a Bowery car to Mott street. For it was raining, and the wind came in fitful gusts that made the protection of a silk umbrella far from perfect.

I decided to brave the elements and trudged toward and across Mail street. Behind the stone breast work stood the familiar "Otis" mail wagons, painted in patriotic colors. The drivers were shoving and tossing, in and out, their complement of mail bags, and were very wet and grouty and uncomfortable. The horses stood wide between the feet, as though braced against the dejection that showed itself in their drooping manes, and tails, and ears. Through the partly open door of the scale shed came the rollicking voices of the mail weighers, and wreaths of blue tobacco smoke floated out and merged themselves into the humid atmosphere.

Across on Park Row a mist overhung the charred ruins of the old *World* building, and Eugene Kelly's gigantic unfinished "Temple Court" upreared its succession of solid stories like a sneering monument to the victims of the fire-trap its late neighbor. The street

cars with sweating windows, with their dual crews clad
in rubber coats, rolled plashing by and were over well
filled.

From the elevated railway station the water poured
in dismal cascades. The fussy little engine of the
shuttle connecting with Chatham square was blowing
off steam. The dimly lighted vista of Chatham street
appeared a gloomy funnel. It often proves so to the
unwary, with the broad end at Chatham square opening on destruction, which is in the Bowery, and radi-
ates therefrom in a dozen different by-ways.

The Chatham street funnel's sides are not intact, however, there are various pitfalls for the innocent and
foolish. Up from a "dive" from which ascended the
discordant strains of a broken piano and cracked violin
came two man-of-war's men. They evidently thought
they were on the rolling deep, and tacked down the
street at a gait that suggested their having their sea
legs on.

"Oh! excuse me, madam."

I had run against a woman while eyeing the pictur-
esque Jack tars. A woman! No, not that, but
one of those evil things which horrify you, accustomed
to the streets of New York by night as well as you
may be.

Ragged and bedraggled with mud, she seemed a
spirit of the night, with the talons of a fury; she first
begged of, and then abused me, passing quickly to the
second experiment of acquiring the price of a dram,
before she proved the first test, as though she was accustomed to failure. A five cent nickel coin was successfully plied as an exorcising medium, but the memory of her face could not be got rid of so easily.

I passed a basement below Mott Street, on Chatham
Square, with the Chinese name of Quong War over its
portal. The door was open, and although a sign set
forth that it was a general tea and provision store, a
strange smell of smoking was wafted up on the foul
warm air. It was the first cloud of incense to the opium

God, who mutely rules the destinies of the inhabitants of Chinatown.

In the entrance to a saloon at the corner of Mott street, stood, waiting for me, a fair-faced young man with a sparse corn-colored moustache. The lower lids of his eyes were inflamed, and of a light red color. His salutation was cordial, and his voice was low, the tones being exquisitely modulated.

This young man was a "fiend." He had a beautiful and accomplished wife and two little children in his tenement home. They were there almost without the necessaries of life, and will probably never receive more than sufficient to relieve their immediate wants from the husband and father, although there is no doubt that he loves them dearly.

I have heard a quondam sojourner in Paris say that he once wandered into what he supposed was a narrow street, in a region surrounded by business thoroughfares, but where the *canaille* seemed also remarkably familiar with the surroundings. It proved a "no thoroughfare," a veritable *cul de sac*, but the curious intruder walked on, surveying the ricketty surroundings, coated with the grime of indescribable poverty, with no small degree of interest.

Strange faces began to appear at broken windows, and he was stared at. Grotesque, but repulsive figures emerged from ruined doorways behind him, and he was gibbered and gabbled at, in the *pa'ois* of the social pariahs. But the gathering behind him of a group of beings, so brutal, depraved, and ferocious, that he failed to discover one sign of the nobler attributes of humanity about them, suggested the advisability of a retreat, and being an old soldier, he knew where to merge valor into discretion and made good his escape.

There are shapes and features, and voices, as strange in Mott, and Park, and Pell streets of a night and more outlandish Malays, Portuguese, or an occasional swarthy sailor from the Levant. Sometimes there is to be seen a Chinese sailor of large frame who seemed

to be akin and yet foreign, to the low statured race of
Kwang Tung coolies around him, who were once, if not
now, the serfs of the Six Companies.

The fiend and the author wended their way up Mott
street.   Three men crouched in the shelter of a door-
way next below Tom Lee's cigar store; Tom is, or was,
a Chinese Deputy Sheriff of New York County; and if
the allegations of numerous of his less shrewd and
more ignorant countrymen are true, he made his official
position pay.   The fitful light from the nearest flicker-
ing street lamp momentarily illuminated their swarthy
faces, and in that instantaneous view enough was seen
of their ill-favored features to warrant the opinion that
they were no company for honest men.   The hard lines
about their mouths expressed a determination to do all
that might be necessary to gratify the cupidity expressed
in their eyes; vicious, depraved, criminal, they were
thievish Thugs of the metropolis ; as crafty and
cruel, when on a sharp scent for plunder, as any wor-
shiper of the goddess Kali who ever trod an Indian
jungle.

The wind increases, and the cold rain beats against
our faces with stinging effect.   Swinging signs and
broken, ricketty shutters—all shutters are broken and
ricketty in Chinatown—creak dismally.   Chinamen
flit noiselessly by in ghostly, fluttering garments, and
startle the Caucasian intruder by the very suddenness
of their unsympathetic companionship.   We see no other
white men in the haunts of these imported Orientals.
The police of the Sixth Precinct do not, to the
author's knowledge, waste many of their nocturnal gold-
en moments in Mott street.

And down below almost every house on either side of
the way for two blocks are the dens of the opium
smokers.   The Chinese manipulators of the *yen hauck*
burrow as far beneath air and light as is possible.
With the exception of accommodating laundry men,
and one Chin Tin, who ventured to start a first floor
joint at No. 48 First street, there is scarcely an instance

where the Chinese worshipers of the pipe can be met
with on the surface.

With my companion I crossed to the west side of the
narrow, ill-flavored street. When we had again come
nearly to Chatham street, he turned on his heel and
suddenly disappeared below ground, I taking the
"dive" after him.

CHAPTER II.

"HITTING THE FLUTE."

ALL the professions have their idiomatic phrases. Opium smoking soon becomes a profession, for one cannot
long remain an amateur in its exercise. Therefore I
shall not apologize for the title of this chapter, in ap-
prehension of the critical reader regarding it as
"slangy." The Chinese—at least in the vernacular of
the smokers who speak the Kwang tung dialect— call
the pipe *Yen Tsiang,* meaning literally "opium pistol,"
and our predecessors in this rapidly-spreading soul-
destroying vice, the San Francisco "hoodlums" saw in it a
nearer resemblance to a flute, and called it accordingly.

"Hello! Sing," said the "fiend," while the author
was rubbing his head where he had struck it against
the top of the low door-way, and closed the heavy door
behind him.

The proprietor, an oval-faced Chinaman inclined to
obesity, came forward shaking hands with himself
and smiling blandly as he bowed, and replied :

"Hello! Flank." His pronunciation showed that
he had not yet become enabled to curl his tongue
around the English consonant "r." The author followed his companion and Sing through a door in a pine
partition, which latter had also a small window in it
like a ticket-seller's. In the large room in which they
found themselves there were lying a dozen Chinamen
on the different wide bunks, or rather on the shelves,

" Shall we smoke a few pipes before we go ?" I asked
my companion.   He assented and we removed our hats,
top and under coats, and even unbuttoned our vests, for
the atmosphere was not only close and impure, but it
was oppressively warm. Frank crawled up on the bunk,
and lay down on his right side, crosswise of the shelf,
resting his head on a cushioned stool placed there for the
purpose.   I crawled up in front of him and lazily laid
my head upon his shirt bosom.

A cadaverous Chinamau with a pock-marked face
presently appeared with a lay-out. Tun Gee was not
an attractive specimen, and his face, upon which I had
never looked before, reminded me just enough of a certain Chinese leper I had once seen in a Pell street den to
send an involuntary shiver of horror over me.

" What's the matter ?" inquired Frank, who had observed the tremor. Tun Gee had gone to another shelf
for a head stool, and I told him in a whisper.

" Pshaw!" he exclaimed, " Tun is all right, he's one
of the best natured Chinamen I know, and is a thoroughly good cook."

Tun Gee crawled up on the bunk with his barbaric
pillow, and also reclined.   There was not much of the
oriental " Beau Brummel" about Tun Gee.   His blue
" jumper" was torn and soiled, and his pig-tail, which
was coiled up and knotted on his shaven head, was not
neatly plaited, and wild hairs stuck out from it sug-
gestive of quills upon the proverbial fretful porcupine.
However, the Chinese New Year's was not far off, when,
consolatory thought, such as he anoint their locks for
the whole ensuing year, and spend much time in plait-
ing anew their queues.

There was nothing to separate my face from Tun
Gee's, which was in close proximity, but the lay-out.

The most noticeable article on the lacquer tray which
the cook had brought was a small glass lamp, two-thirds
full of peanut oil, something like a large goblet, with
a hole where the stem of the pedestal would have joined
the cup, was inverted over the lamp for a globe, and

the flame just reached the hole.   The air entered through scallops in the edge of the globe and thus made an equal draft all around the flame and kept it steady.

A miniature China jar, which would hold about two fluid ounces, called the *hop toy*, contained the opium, called *opien* by the Chinese.   A small bowl held the ash; the latter is called *yen t^hi*.   A straight steel wire, the size of a knitting needle, with one end flattened, is termed the *yen hauck*.   This was used for taking up the opium, kneading it, and rolling it about while it is cooking.   A sponge kept in a small bowl, and partially saturated with water, was used to clean the broad face of the pipe bowl.

Last and largest of all the implements comprised in the lay-out was the pipe itself, called in Chinese *yen tsiang*.   The stem of this particular pipe was twenty-four inches long, and over an inch in diameter.   It was of bamboo, and the mouth-piece was the same in size as the rest of the stem.   About eighteen inches from the mouth-piece was the bowl, which was shaped like a shallow bell, with a smooth face instead of a mouth.   The opening in this pipe bowl would scarcely admit an ordinary knitting needle, it being even smaller than the average.

Tun Gee lay upon his left, and the white fiend and myself—the neophyte—upon our right sides.   Tun Gee picked up the *yen hauck*, twisted it several times about in the viscid dark mass in the *hop toy*, as a glass-blower would twist his pipe in the molten glass to secure a lump of the raw material, and then held it over the flame, slowly twirling the slender steel, as the opium fused and seemed about to run in drops into the lamp.

"Is not that a beautiful golden brown?" purred the fiend in his gentle tones.   It was.   The boiling mass seemed filled with a maze of golden threads.   It was a fascinating operation, enhanced by the impatient expectancy of shortly entering the seventh heaven of the opium smoker's delight.

It was a weird, uncanny scene. The cadaverous visage of Tun Gee; the inflamed and drooping eyelids of the fiends—who both seemed to reflect from their eyes the latent fierce desire to transform those twining gold threads into the smoke, which was to transport us all lightly into the anticipated elysium. But as all three knew, as well to forge new links of steel, which would remain when the threads of gold were gone, and adding, make the fetters of habit more binding.

The consistent mass was then placed against the face of the bowl, rolled and kneaded, and tried again in the fire till it assumed the semblance of a pill. The point of the steel then pierced the pill and passed through it into the bowl.

Tun Gee grinned in ghastly, quiet satisfaction. As the *chef* of the Hotel Brunswick might smile over a successful dish to which he had given his personal superintendence, so did the chief cook of the Mott street joint express his petty triumph in his art. He covered the patron fiend with the muzzle of the opium pistol, and my companion eagerly grasped it.

His lips closed around the thick clumsy stem, and he took a long draw, holding the face of the bowl with its adhering opium slant-wise over the flame, Tun Gee, meanwhile kneading the consuming drug with the *yen hauck*. Several short puffs supplemented the long draw and the pipe was out.

"That was a good pipe, Tun," approvingly muttered the fiend; Tun Gee grinned in response and applied himself to preparing my dose of poison. Lifting my head, which I rested on my right hand, and holding the unwieldy pipe in my left, I followed the fiend's example. I restored the pipe to Tun Gee, and then I saw what was enough to deter any man from smoking in Chinatown. Tun Gee proceeded to hit the pipe himself.

The bamboo or lemon peel stem of an opium pipe, when passed in short succession from lip to lip, must be a not infrequent conveyance of disease. An efficient ally is it in extending the sway of that arch-enemy to the bones and tissues, Syphilis.

Dr. H. H. Kane has already noted three such cases, two of which he treated himself. Another unpleasant —to say the very least—feature of smoking in the Chinatown of New York, although it is rare as yet, compared to the Chinatown of San Francisco, is the chance of meeting a leper in the "joints."

It is accepted by the disciples of Esculapius as a fact that *elephantiasis græcorum* is but hereditary and not contagious. Nevertheless, the disease and its miserable victims are both as abhorrent to healthy humanity to-day as they were in the days when the Nazarene compassionately cured that unclean one of Galilee.

The Tartar coolie who ekes out a miserable subsistence by cooking opium, takes his alternate smoke as much as a matter of course as a waiter at Delmonico's would accept his "tip." Were it not for this privilege he might summon up sufficient energy to work in a laundry or make cigars, and after all only to deposit the product of his labor with the joint-keeper for opium.

After my companion, myself and Tun Gee had consumed fifty cents worth, being somewhere between 75 and 100 grains, Tun Gee sponged the pipe-bowl for the last time. I felt loth to leave, and did so, only after considerable effort, feeling delightfully at peace with myself and all the world.

CHAPTER III.

WOMEN WHO SMOKE.

THE opium pipe has a terrible fascination for the weaker sex. Women have become addicted to liquor and have remained otherwise pure; in fact, if not in heart. They have used tobacco, and retained their womanly qualities still, although assuredly with a loss of refinement.   They have eaten arsenic for their complexion without contracting other vicious habits, except, perhaps, the sequent one of lying to conceal it, and they have even used morphine hypodermically, or internally, and remained virtuous.   But where is the woman who can continue to smoke opium in the joints and preserve her chastity ?

The female " fiend " to be found in the joints of New York is not of the same species as the old hag in London, whom Charles Dickens describes " John Jasper" as visiting in his "Mystery of Edwin Drood." Nor—it may be here remarked—does Dickens' description of opium smoking apply to the vice as it presently exists in the United States.   The women who smoke are almost without exception under thirty years of age.   A majority of those whom I have observed are under twenty-one years.   As the habit only became extended beyond the practice of a few individual Americans on the Pacific slope ten years ago, in two decades more there are likely to be some old hags visible in the joints.   It will be the survival of the strongest, if not the fittest.   Social opium smoking, with its accompanying or consequent habits, is not conducive to longevity in woman.

The class of women, or girls, who frequent the joints, are usually those who may be found at the " Sixth avenue dives " and kindred resorts on Bleecker street, or the Bowery; also variety actresses, and some whose names are widely known in the legitimate drama. There are also a few young women, who usually come in carriages, who are reticent in all conversation tending to show curiosity about their identity or social relations, but who, nevertheless, join freely in the delightful *conversaziones* on general subjects, which the *olla podrida* nature of the society to be met with in a metropolitan opium den, never fail to make entertaining, and even fascinating.   I have been assured, with mystery and pride, by the fiends that these were representatives of the real upper tendom.

The best of the female society constantly to be met
with in the joints are those plainly designated as
"kept women"—those frail ones who hover on the
boundaries of the *demi monde* by living on the bounty
of rich men, while bestowing their genuine caresses on
worthless but handsome rogues, who laugh with them
at their rivals, and help to spend the lavishly bestowed
dollars of the men who pay.

To this class of women belongs a character, so well
known to the frequenters of the New York dens, that
they cannot fail to recognize the following pen picture
however unskillfully the author may have drawn it.
My first meeting with "Viola Hardinge," as she is
generally known to the smokers, was in one of the
ornate and luxurious "joints" latterly started by an
American. It was a late hour of a cold night, and a
hard coal fire burning in a nickel fronted grate beneath
a costly marble mantel, made the opium palace a much
cosier place than palatial halls are wont to be.

There were nearly two dozen smokers stretched at
length or curled up enwrapped in sweet idleness, on
divans overlaid with soft Smyrna rugs. Their tones
were—as ever—low and sweet, and the gentle harmony
of their weird social intercourse was never more apparent. We heard the tinkle of the door bell, and a
moment later the door to the joint opened, and a female
figure attired in satin and heavy furs appeared. The
cold draught from the hall sent a momentary chill down
my back, and I heard through the distant front door,
before it was softly closed by the Chinese attendant, a
carriage rattle noisily away through the frosty air, echo-
ing loudly in the hitherto quiet street.

"*Sacristi!* But it's Viola," exclaimed a man, with
hair falling long and luxuriant over his shoulders, whom
the apparition in black had aroused from his pleasant
meditations.

"Air yez shure it uz, noo?" queried the new comer
in the shrill weak querulous voice of an old Irish crone.
The votaries of the opium pipe slowly lifted themselves,

and with unusual activity some six or seven actually
summoned up sufficient energy to leave their places,
and gather around the coming accession to their reclining ranks, reminding me of nothing so much as
"The mild-eyed melancholy Lotos-Eaters came."

Viola removed her wraps, which she negligently tossed
into the arms of one of her subjects (she was sometimes
fancifully termed the "Queen of the Joint"), who, as
"Master of the Robes," carefully hung them up at the
other end of the palace. Then the girl or woman—I
could scarcely tell which—lightly scaled the somewhat
inconvenient height of the divan, and accepting a cigarette from another girl, reclining beside her, pushed a
small foot and neat ankle, encased in a high-laced fur-
topped boot, over the edge of the divan, and said to one
of the fiends, "George, have the kindness to unlace
that, there's a good fellow."

George entered upon his task in a very matter of fact
way, and removed both of her shoes, being apparently
sufficiently rewarded by a very gracious acknowledg-
ment of her obligations by Viola.

Meanwhile I stared lazily at "Her Majesty," but
was in too careless a mood after having disposed of a
dozen or so pipes, to speculate freely, and only vaguely
wondered at the time who she might be. It was not
altogether her personal appearance that made her the
centre of attraction, but her physique was good ; although her figure was small it was well-rounded and
proportioned. Her hair was a chestnut brown, and
her eyes bluish grey. There was but little color in her
cheeks, notwithstanding she came so lately from the
bracing outer air. The redness and inflammation in
her lower eyelids were less observable than in many of
the other fiends, of either sex. Her voice, when speaking, had a dry unmusical sound, but could not be called
harsh, nevertheless she afterward proved to be a very
entertaining vocalist.

This then is a description of the woman who was
called the "Queen," among the slaves of the pipe. It

is certainly not a fanciful picture of a beauty. Nor
was there anything of the capricious belle about Viola,
and she seemed to have her friends and admirers equally
divided between the male and female smokers.

Superiority of intellect, tact, a happy and fluent expression in relating incidents of her travels and varied
experiences ; a knack of telling humorous stories in a
way to get the best effect; a certain degree of dramatic
power and musical accomplishments, of which she could
only exhibit her vocal powers in the joints, were the
reasons why Viola was pre-eminent in a company, where
the majority were intellectual and well-informed, and
all had need to be amused.

The girl, with the freedom born, not of the life of
shame she had led, so much as of the peculiar unsexing
influence of the joints, loosed the laces of her *vetement pour
le taille*, and with her little feet (almost as small, though
not like them, cruelly misshapen, as those of the Chinese
women, whose national vice she had chosen to be her
darling sin), encased in dainty silken hose, visible beyond the hem of her dress and jutting over the edge of
the divan, lay cooking her own opium.

One of the fiends, a man with a pleasant face and en-
gaging, though melancholy manner, lounged noiselessly
along the aisle over the soft rich carpeting, and stood
regarding her a moment.

" Won't you cook for me, Viola? you know your
cooking is just to my taste," he said in a gentle,
plaintive voice.

" Why, cert'! come on Charley, one would almost
think you had just returned from the wholesale burying
of all your friends," said the girl, laughing at his plaintive tone, and Charley crawled up on the divan, and
comfortably bestowed his head upon an inflated rubber pillow.

The stories and jokes which flowed in rapid succession
from the " Queen's " lips shortly had the effect of not
only developing an unsuspected—to me—depth of humor
in "Charley" himself, but of enlivening all the smokers

immediately about the pair. With the obliging fiend,
who was cooking for us both, I went to where Viola lay.
Two or three others had left their pipes, and seated
themselves on the edge of the divan near her feet.
Viola passed some fragrant cigarettes of Turkish tobacco
around the circle, and the *converzazione* there instituted
was entertaining, and to some extent instructive. There
was nothing said to offend the ear polite. There did,
however, very frequently occur slang expressions peculiar to the fraternity of "crooks" who were represented
in the party.

Afterward I learned something of Viola's history,
which in detail would be a theme for the pen of a Zola,
although the bitter end is not yet,

"The Hardinge" was a daughter of the middle class
in an interior small city. The class which is in culture
and manner the true aristocracy of this country.
Bright, vivacious, and winning, she was a leader among
her companions, and was sought after by young men
when she was still a girl in years. Her precocious intellect outran her judgment and she withdrew her confidence from her mother to put her trust in a fascinating and brilliant rogue. She got left. This terse sentence condenses several bitter, heart-rending chapters
in Viola's biography.

After that, being too proud to return home, she saw
but the one career of wickedness open to her and on that
broad ladder she ascended upon the extravagant favor of
western men to the top rung. A very few years ago, it is
said, she was at the head of a large establishment in
St. Louis, where she was yclept the "Kid Madame,"
because of her obvious youth. There the second object upon whom she had bestowed her affections was
arrested for murder. She mortgaged her house for
$14,000, and eventually saved him from being hanged :
but she expended her last dollar in his behalf with a
devotion worthy of a better cause. She was afterwards a local celebrity in Deadwood, where she kept a
miners' boarding house, and it is related that she was

charitably inclined, having entertained and sheltered
gratuitously various "tender-feet" who were "dead
broke." She lived in style in a San Francisco hotel,
and subsequently travelled "around the world."

Viola began to smoke opium in Nevada and has since
smoked in joints and laundries wherever she found
them. Since her debut in Gotham she has always lived
and dressed well, and is a profitable patron of the
ultra-fashionable Turkish Baths, being a connoisseur in
that borrowed Oriental luxury.

A woman who would marry a Chinaman—not the
Chinamen we have seen and heard of as diplomatically
representing the "Flowery Kingdom" at Washington,
or the *jeunesse doree* from Victoria or Canton, who have
studied at Yale, but such a one as is to be found in a
Chinatown grocery or a laundry—must be at the very
lowest notch of the social scale. There are many such,
however, and with the exception of an occasional German, they are Irish, and in contracting such *mesalli-
ances*, they unaccountably turn traitor to a prejudice so
often expressed by their compatriots, that it may fairly
be termed a national one.

Ellen Doyle was one of these. She had been brought
up in the atmosphere of the Five Points—as they were
—which may be an excuse. She lived with her husband in a Mott street rookery, and became, like him,
a devoted opium smoker. Latterly she left him, and
has since lived with her mother on Pell street, near the
Bowery, which is no great remove, either in point of
linear distance, or degrees of the social scale.

The victims of opium are notably terrible liars about
their habit, but the story that Ellen told was of a remarkable cure which may have some factitious elements,
although its permanency is yet to be proven. She said
she sometimes smoked frequently during a single day,
and never abstained from it altogether during any single
day, unless she had no money to obtain it, she at such
times enduring agonies of craving.

Being finally thoroughly disgusted and ashamed, she

determined to quit visiting the joints in the neighborhood of her husband's home, and provided herself with a quantity of opium, which she rolled into pills. These she took daily, intending to decrease the quantity very gradually, but in five or six days she realized with joyful surprise that she was not suffering at all, and ceased taking the pills altogether.

The first day that she went without, she was ill with some of the usual symptoms consequent on abstinence from the drug, but the second day she did not miss it, and claims to have never since conceived a desire to resume its use.

The "fake" museum on the western side of Chatham square, with its brilliant lights, its gaudily painted impossible show pictures, and the old man who mutely but expressively points to them with his cane, in the hope of winning some rural stranger with the promise delineated on the canvas, with its hangers on, including "faro steerers" and "hand-shakers," one of whom is, or was, a quondam pal of " Dutch Heinrich's "—a gentleman ? well known to the Central Office detective force—is a familiar institution to all who pass that way after gaslight.

There was for a long time a girl or woman there who performed the once famous, but long since exposed, "Sphinx" trick, under the resonant title of "The Herodian Mystery "—her head being exhibited upon a platter on a table, apparently minus a trunk. Her husband had charge of a cage which contained a mangy and sickly looking "happy family," comprising specimens of some of the smaller animals.

The husband had been for six years or more an opium smoker, and for half that time an inebriate. The woman had also smoked opium for several years. Both frequented the joints in Chinatown, and almost always together. Their engagement having terminated at the place above mentioned, they, encouraged by Dr. Kane, went to the De Quincey Home, at Fort Washington, and by his treatment were, as they and he believed, cured.

Delia frequently takes Barney to task for his extravagance, but woe betide him, if he does not "produce" the cash she asks for, when *she* is in the notion of having a little expensive excitement, even though the amount be in the hundreds of dollars.

One Winter's night in the joint then kept by Matt Grace—the wrestler, who is now dead—next to the rear of Niblo's Garden, on Crosby street, a fiend in full evening dress, who had dropped in after attending a ball at the Academy of Music, sat cross legged on the edge of the bunk, reading from the *New York Tribune* as follows; the fiends listening intently the while, although their eyes twinkled, and they seemed trying hard to repress their emotions.

"A ROW IN AN OPIUM DEN."

"Delia Maguire, a fashionably dressed young woman, was arraigned in the Essex Market Police Court, yesterday, charged on complaint of Elizabeth Chin Tin, the wife of a Chinaman, with disorderly conduct. From the evidence of the complainant it appeared that the prisoner came to her house, at No. 48 First street, late on Saturday night, and after raising much disturbance, broke a show case containing cigars. In testifying in her own defense, the prisoner stated that her husband, Barney Maguire, was addicted to the use of opium, and that on Saturday night she learned that he was smoking the drug at Chin Tin's place. She accordingly went there for the purpose of taking her husband home, but was resisted in her attempt by the wife of the Chinaman. An altercation ensued, which was followed by a struggle, in the course of which the show-case was accidentally shattered. In rendering a decision in the case, Justice White said that Mrs. Maguire was justified in following the course that she had adopted. In his opinion the opium dens in this city were evils, which called loudly for oppression. The magistrate then dismissed the case."

When the reader finished, the fiends laughed immoderately, and one of them said he had gone over to Essex Market to hear the examination. He said that his honor, Judge White, and the court officers seemed to sympathize deeply with the unfortunate Mrs. Maguire, whose husband was a victim to the awful habit of opium smoking. As for Mrs Chin Tin, she was regarded in the court with horror and aversion

Delia, who is almost as much of a fiend as Barney himself, laughed till she cried when safely beyond the ken of the court, at the way in which she had acquired a character at the expense of the worsted Mrs. Chin Tin. The truth of it all was that Delia was on one of her periodical rampages and that Mrs. Chin Tin, who knew her sufficiently well, perceived that she was about to "run a muck" through all the breakable articles of furniture in the joint, and with notable loyalty to her squint-eyed, pig-tailed husband, threw herself into the imminent and deadly breach in time to prevent it.

The "women who smoke," while they discuss freely their habit and its effects with the other fiends, do not, through shame or policy, usually confide the fact of their indulgence to others. They find it necessary or advisable to keep an extra suit of garments for wear in the opium den, as every stitch of their clothing becomes impregnated with the odor, which, like tobacco smoke, becomes strong and rank when stale. When they can afford it, they always arrange to have a cab call for them, because they are only too well aware that their persons and clothing are redolent of the smoke, and it often causes comment and remark in a street or elevated railway car, even though none of the passengers may know what it is

It may be said here that there is something so peculiar, and it would seem fascinating, about the lingering smell of burning or burnt opium, that the person whose olfactories it greets for the first time is seldom satisfied with mere speculation as to its origin. This the author remembers very clearly in his own experi-

ence, when he deposited his own undergarments in the
family wash at home, after his first night among the
fiends, and the perplexity that the odor occasioned
"Bridget."

After once smoking opium the sense of smell is
keenly susceptible to it, and it is a matter of fact that
after a long absence from the joints and losing all
knowledge of Chin Tin's whereabouts after his disappearance from First street, the author discovered his
subterranean den at No. 9 Bowery, while walking up
that thoroughfare with a journalistic friend, by the odor
which stole up through the cellar grating.

The last clause in this chapter shall be but a brief
mention of a horrible truth. It was used as the strongest argument for immediate action in the Legislatures of
California and Nevada. Among the men who are old
and adept in the arts of villainy, as well as that of smoking opium, are some who have not hesitated to entice
virtuous women and girls into the joints. Upon many
females smoking opium acts as a most powerful aphro-
disiac, and thus their moral ruin quickly overtakes
them, but not more certainly than their physical destruction will be accomplished sooner or later by the
same cause.

It was early in the month of May, 1883, and after
the M S. for this volume was in the hands of my print-
ers, that a young girl named Emma Pool, of No. 6
Bayard street, came to the railing in the Tombs Police
Court, and asked Justice Kilbreth for a warrant
for the arrest of Mrs. Elizabeth Chin Tin, of No. 94
Pell street, the Irish wife of a degraded Chinaman.
The girl was sallow of complexion, and her eyes were
red. She grasped the railing with both hands, but her
arms moved nervously.

"What makes you tremble so?" asked the justice in
a not unkind tone.

"Opium smoking," was the reply.

The girl said her habit had been growing for over
three years. She accused the woman of dosing chil-

dren with opium concealed in candy, and gave the names of three girls, none of them over 15 years of age, who visited her almost daily, while their parents believed them to be at work. Justice Kilbreth issued a warrant, and instructed a sergeant-detective and an officer of the Society for the Prevention of Cruelty to Children to execute it.

I had long ago brought the chapter descriptive of "Women Who Smoke," with its incidental mention of Mrs. Chin Tin, during her short but stormy residence with her husband on First street, to a close, with the general statement of "a horrible truth." Within a fortnight hundreds of revolting details in evidence of that statement have been published in the metropolitan press.

The Chinatown proper of New York city is bounded on the North by Bayard street, on the East and South by the Bowery and Chatham square, and on the West by Pearl and Centre streets, although but a few outlying spurs of the great celestial colony extend to the latter broad thoroughfare. Right in the midst of this congregation of heathens, at Mott and Park streets, stands the Roman Catholic Church of the Transfiguration.

I have myself seen the worshipers walking into its portals, missal and breviary in hand, with reverent mien, as the mellow tones of the old bell summoned the believers to vespers, while it was all that I could do to push through the hordes of Pagans, and vile off-scourings of all Christian nations, who were holding a carnival of crime, and not half trying to hide it, in and in front of the swarming tenements they infested. I saw and felt this as well as did the new Sixth Precinct policeman who strolled lazily along, dexterously twirling an ornamental truncheon hung to his wrist by a cord of crimson silk. But neither the policeman nor myself had our attention arrested by such an unusual sight as Chinese proselytes mingling the patter of their wooden soled shoes with the march of the faithful in search of the comforts of Christianity.

Of course, when a church contributes to the general foreign mission fund its very respectable quota, it could hardly be expected that its members should do, without getting off their own door steps, what they are paying the black-gowns to do in far off Cathay.

At No. 20 Mott street, nearly across from the church, the Young Men's Association connected with it have their rooms. Suddenly the members of this organization had their eyes opened to the enormity of the evil hemming them in, and threatening the virtue and blasting the future of even their little sisters. Young blood will tell. It is hot when its owner is wounded in a spot that involves the honor and delicacy of a brother's love for a sister, and as the wicked Chinamen and more wicked white women discovered, the hell fires of immorality they had kindled suddenly burst forth in retribution upon themselves. The young men held meetings. There was much enthusiasm. It was decided to call upon the societies for the Suppression of Vice, for the Prevention of Crime and for the Prevention of Cruelty to Children, to aid them in the work, as well as to send circulars to the prominent clergymen of all denominations throughout the city, inviting them to attend their meetings and to co-operate with them in rooting out the opium-dens.

The police were last thought of, and with some creditable exceptions were contemptuously referred to as having "known all about it long enough without ever doing anything." Then certain charges by Chinese keepers of opium-dens and gambling houses, before Mr. Anthony Comstock, Superintendent of the Society for the Suppression of Vice, were recalled as having been made against Tom Lee, the Chinese ex-Special Deputy Sheriff ; cigar dealer ; restaurant keeper; real estate owner, and generally the great Mongolian magnate of Mott street. These allegations were that he, in connection with some police officer in citizen's clothes, had levied a constant blackmail on the evil doers. It was alleged by the awful array of pig-tailed accusers, who uprose against the short-haired Tom, that one gambling house which refused to pay its "license for gambling purposes" had been " pulled " by the police.

Mr. Lee is one of the longest-headed Chinamen—although comparatively uneducated — on the Alantic slope. When the reporters interviewed him he replied with a smiling indifference, in the form of a general denial, or referred them to his counsel, and he was shrewd enough and could well afford to get a good one.

Thus by inference the finger of suspicion of at least neglect of duty, if not worse, veered toward the station of the Sixth Precinct Police in Elizabeth street.

On the evening of May 7th, the Young Men's Association met and adopted the following resolution:—

"Whereas, for the last few years this locality has been selected as the spot whereon to open in this city, by the side of the houses of the poor, brothels and houses of ill-fame to pander to the licentiousness of a class of people who have no homes or family ties of their own; and, whereas, the growth of this evil has been so rapid, and the efforts to prevent it so feeble, that it becomes necessary for self-protection to adopt some measures more efficacious to remedy the evil and render a residence here possible to those who respect virtue and decency; therefore, be it

Resolved, That a special committee of five members of this association be appointed to wait on the police authorities of this city and the presidents of the societies for the Prevention of Crime and for the Prevention of Cruelty to Children and ask their help in their efforts to remove one of the most revolting evils that has existed in the city of New York.

The president, Mr. William H. Smith, said, while one of the priests of the Church of the Transfiguration was walking through Mott street on the previous night he was struck and grossly insulted by an abandoned girl from one of the Chinese dens. He called attention to the wholesale ruin of young girls by Chinamen in that neighborhood, of which the members of the association were well aware, and declared that there was scarcely a house between the association rooms and Chatham square that was not either an opium den or a house of ill-fame.

Father Barry, the honorary president, made an elaborate speech, in which he said that every citizen ought to give his assistance in exterminating the evil which was undermining the morals and destroying the virtue of the community.

"It is an insupportable idea," he exclaimed, "that these pagan barbarians can carry on their horrible orgies right among us, corrupt our children and convert our peaceable neighborhood into a hotbed of crime and debauchery. They are destroying the daughters of respectable parents by an organized system. We will call to our aid all the power of the existing authorities and root out the evil at once. We will say nothing now of those who we know must aid and abet these dens of iniquity, for it might frustrate our purpose. But if the authorities fail to move, and if those whom we believe to be the supporters of these crimes do not help us and do their duty, we will investigate from the bottom to the top, and we will give their names to the world."

The committee appointed in accordance with the resolution included John A. O'Brien, Thomas H. Morse, Michael Frazer, Patrick H. McDonnell and Patrick Callahan.

Then followed a series of arrests of young girls and Chinamen. The Tombs Police Court was crowded at every hearing, and the papers, with the notable exception of the *Times*, devoted from a half column to three columns in their daily issues to the results of this new crusade. Mr. Jenkins, the superintendent of the Society for the Prevention of Cruelty to Children, investigated one or two of the cases thoroughly and then made the rather broad declaration that there was little or nothing in the whole of the sweeping charges against the Chinamen.

Father Lynch, at the head of the Church of the Transfiguration, was reported as deprecating Father Barry's action in the matter, and asserted that the movement was not authorized by the church. The chairman of the association's special committee, Mr. John A. O'Brien, subsequently stated at one of their public meetings, that they were not moving as Catholics but as citizens.

Neither was the Chinese side of the question unheard.

A number of conspicuous Chinamen, principally merchants, met in the *Chinese-American* office in Chatham street to discuss the charges that the association has preferred against their people. Messrs. Wong and Charles of the Chinese newspaper acted as chairman and secretary respectively, and Mr. Wong Chin Foo introduced the subject in a vigorous address. He denounced in severe terms the conduct of those New York newspapers that had made it appear that all the Chinese in the city were guilty of the immoralities in question. "We would have been grateful," he said, "if those newspapers had mentioned by name whatever individual Chinamen are known to have willfully committed the heinous crime of enticing to ruin the innocent children of their neighbors. It appears, however, to have been too much trouble for them to find out the particulars, and so, with one sweeping assertion they charge this terrible crime upon the entire Chinese community. It is a thing too serious, too cruel, too relentless to be endured without being met by some action by those who are innocent."

It was resolved that the minutes of the meeting should be published in the next issue of the Chinese newspaper, and further, that all present should diligently aid the authorities in bringing the guilty parties to justice, whatever the expense might be and by whatever means they possess.

It was said that an announcement of this determination had already been sent by the chairman "to the officers having charge of such matters." The meeting lasted from eight o'clock in the evening until nearly one o'clock in the morning. Mr. Wong Chin Foo said that in a few days the public might expect to see the fruits of the work thus set on foot.

Beside this demonstration on Saturday, May 12th, a deputation of about thirty of the most respectable Chinese inhabitants of the city entered Colonel Charles S. Spencer's office, in the *Tribune* building, to consult with him and Mr. Charles Myers, their legal counsel, as to the best means they could adopt to break up the opium dens. They said they realized the harm it was doing them in their legitimate trade and occupations, and were anxious that the sheep should be separated from the goats among their nationality in the eyes of the Americans. Several of them are the same who a short time before threw off the yoke alleged to have been illegally imposed upon them by Tom Lee and his associates.

The editorial comments upon this new crusade were many and various. I select the *Herald's* to lead, because it is the most comprehensive, and because it embodies the first thought that entered my mind. when the excitement over the revelations in Chinatown began to effervesce. This was, that the voice of the press and people of the Pacific Slope would exultingly remind us of the East, " We told you so; now you know how it is yourselves."

(*From the Herald.*)

THE MOTT STREET REVELATIONS.

The iniquities practiced by some members of the Chinese colony in Mott street appear not to have been overstated by Father Barry in his recent charges. There may be different views as to the amount of physical and moral harm done, for Mr. Jenkins, of the Society for the Prevention of Cruelty to Children, aaid in court yesterday that he would prove there was " nothing in it ;" whereas he signified to a *Herald* reporter that he had a list almost as long as his arm of very young girls who had been lured into the opium dens and ruined. Why the society which so savagely runs down small bicycle riders and little chorus singers should allow the wholesale debauchery of young girls to go on for years, although knowing of it all the while, is not apparent. Among a certain class of philanthropists there is a theory that some people are born to become vicious and depraved, and might as well be ruined by Chinamen as by others ; perhaps some of the society's officers have taken refuge in this dismal belief. Why the police have not interfered was explained when the Chinese gamblers said that they had paid money to secure immunity. The ways of the police in overlooking the sins of very sinful neighborhoods are pretty generally understood by this time.

When the *Herald* of yesterday and to-day reaches San Francisco there will probably be some unseemly but natural exultation in the anti-Chinese party. "Now the East will know how it is themselves," will be the general remark, and it will be made without the slightest trace of sympathy. Well there is some similarity in the cases, and in New York as in San Francisco, the general public and its officials are almost as guilty as the Chinese. The incursion of any large body of foreigners, all men and of low moral and intellectual grade and disposed to herd together, is something that no city or country can afford to leave unheeded. Were several hundred of the commonest Americans to gather in a single quarter, a single street, almost a single square, of a Chinese city and be allowed to do just as they pleased so long as they refrained from robbing or murdering the natives, the moral average of the neighborhood would be lowered with great rapidity. Yet San Francisco allowed, and to this day allows, the vilest of her Chinese population to cluster together and considers their unclean doings one of the sights that no stranger should neglect, and New York has followed her example and suffered the inevitable results. In any European city the vicious portion of a colony of aliens would be con-

tinually under police surveillance. In New York the
police seem to inspire terror only as blackmailers do.

Because, however, the eastern end of Mott street is
almost entirely given over to vicious Chinamen and
their unclean ways, just as parts of the Sixth, the
Twenty-ninth and other police precincts are devoted to
indecencies that the Celestials must work hard to surpass,
there is no possible sense in a general tirade against
the Chinese as a class. Beastly Chinamen flock to Mott
street "joints" just as beastly Americans congregate at
Billy McGlory's and similar dens. They cannot have
less pity for youth and ignorance than thousands of men
who were born and reared in the shadow of Christian
churches. There are, however, in the East, as on the
Pacific coast, many thousands of industrious Chinamen
who neither smoke opium nor regard immoral indulgence
as the sole end of life. They came here to earn and save
money with which to return to their country and maintain themselves and their families in comfort, and they
abhor the ways of their dissolute fellow countrymen as
the respectable American in business at Havana, London, Paris or Naples dislikes the doings of the crowds
of young men from this country who devote their attention strictly to whatever is improper and unclean in
those cities.

Nevertheless New York should take warning by this
most recent of her shameful experiences and keep closer
watch upon the localities to which the Chinese resort
for purposes of dissipation. And the work of the law
should be supplemented by that of the Church and of
private societies for the suppression of vice and the protection of the young. The theory that some classes, including many young girls in the tenement districts, are
bound to go to the bad, and if they do not fall in one
place they will in another, should not be tolerated, particularly in philanthropic circles, for these would have
no excuse for existence were this theory correct. Even
among the most determined criminals crime is greatly
lessened by such watchfulness as an efficient police force

can manifest. For the rest the churches and societies claim so much influence that stories like these which come from Mott street should be without excuse for existence.

The comment of the *Herald* is however but the reflection of the intelligent accounts of the American-Chinese troubles in its news columns. The *Herald's* reporter for the inclosed Chinese district is Mr. James Creelman, an enthusiastic aeronaut, and the young gentleman who, as a correspondent for the *Herald*, accompanied Captain Paul Boynton on his tour along the aqueous highways of the country, when exhibiting his natatorial prowess and advertising somebody's patent life-preserving rubber suits.

It is said that these two gentlemen were received, in the interior towns they deigned to honor with their presence, by the mayors and a long retinue of local dignitaries and celebrities. Mr. Creelman seems to have impressed Chinatown, or conquered it with kindness in the same way, for at his advent, even the wealthiest of silk clad Mott street merchants shake both their hands violently, and salaam with the utmost respect. No opium joint exists deep enough under ground to escape the observation and invasion of Mr. Creelman, and he is accredited, by his friends among the reporters, with being able to speak the twenty different dialects of China, sometimes used even in Mott street, with elegant fluency. I do not know this to be true, but I do know that he has a well fund of factitious knowledge from which to draw, where the limited scources of information concerning the local Chinese and their doings available to many a good reporter has forced him into the realms of imagination to fill the space allotted him without "padding."

(From the N. Y. Times.)

A NEW CHARGE.

The excitement over the Chinese infamies in Mott street has in a measure subsided. While the existence of opium smoking haunts among the Mott street China-

meu has been notorious for years, the police know
nothing of the specific and monstrous charges brought
against the Chinamen by the Irish residents of the
neighborhood. Also, an Irish Roman Catholic clergy-
man who resides in the Chinese district professes to be
unable to discover that the Chinamen are corrupting
all the little girls of the ward with "opium candy."
Undoubtedly most of the Irish accusers of the Chinese
firmly believe the preposterous charges that they have
made, but that the charges are preposterous there is
hardly any reason to doubt.

There is, however, an evident desire on the part of
certain enemies of the Chinese to seize the present opportunity to provoke an Irish crusade against the
heathen. Crowds of young "hoodlums" gather in
Mott street and support the cause of morality and
Christianity by throwing stones through the windows
of the houses occupied by Chinamen. It is strange
that the latter, desperate as we are told that they are, do
not draw the knives and revolvers which they all notor-
iously carry in their pockets, and rush out to massacre
their enemies; but, perhaps, they are temporarily stupe-
fied by their own "opium candy." Perhaps, also, they
are made cowards by a knowledge of the truth of a new
charge which has been made against them. It is now
openly and fearlessly asserted that the Mott street Chinamen are habitually guilty of the loathsome practice
of paying their rent, although they are charged enor-
mously high rents for the wretched houses in which they
live. That they should pay their rent is, in the opinion
of the local Irishmen, conclusive proof of their hideous
moral depravity, and it must be confessed that there is
too much reason to believe that this latest charge is
true.

If the Chinamen would see the iniquity of smoking
opium, and would manifest their repentance by buying
rum at the nearest grocery kept by an Irish patriot,
and if they would abandon their habit of earning, by
incessant but cheap labor, money enough to pay their

rent, there would be something to be said in their defense. As it is, their wickedness is glaring, and their windows must be broken if virtue and Christianity are to survive. Had the story of the "opium candy" been circulated more rapidly and judiciously than it was, Irish public sentiment might have been wrought up to the point of exterminating the yellow heathen, but as it is, it is doubtful if the new crusade accomplishes anything of more moment than the breakage of Chinese windows.

(*From the Sun.*)

THE OPIUM JOINTS.

However much or little there may be in the particular charges made against the Chinese quarter, one thing is certain ; the opium joints there are propagating a form of vice which ought to be suppressed.

It is true that before we had any Chinamen in New York there were victims to opium here. Both druggists and physicians tell us that the habitual consumption of opium is lamentably frequent in all parts of the country, and more especially at the East and the West. And the circumstances that cures of the habit are extensively and regularly advertised in the newspapers confirms the truth of what they say regarding the prevalence of the ruinous indulgence. The crude opium, laudanum, and morphine are all consumed in great quantities by victims of the habit. A large part of the demand for opium, in its various forms, comes from them.

But the victims of the opium habit must usually obtain the drug and the preparations of the drug they affect in a more or less stealthy way. They buy it under the pretense that they want it for medicinal purposes only, and to get enough for their satisfaction they may have to go to several druggists, buying a small quantity here and there.

The druggist here, too, is obliged to have a license to sell opium and other drugs, to ask of the buyer what he wants a dangerous drug for, and to enter the exact sale in a book open to inspection. The law could hardly go further toward preventing the supply of opium to habitual consumers, though doubtless in New York, and in very many cities and towns, druggists, for the sake of pecuniary profit, throw few obstacles in the way of the opium drunkard.

The Chinese opium joint, however, is run for the sole purpose of pandering to a vicious taste whose indulgence is injurious to society. More than that, it offers a new temptation to vice, and directly helps to increase the number of the victims of opium, and consequently to swell the horde of paupers and delinquents and to multiply insanity.

So long as it was believed that Chinamen themselves were the only patrons of such dens, the public were little concerned about them. The vice practiced there was an imported one, confined to the comparatively small number of men who brought it over from Asia with them, according to the general supposition.

But it is now charged that these opium joints are drawing in recruits for the host of opium victims from among the inhabitants of the neighborhood who are not Chinese. Very probably the extent of this new development of the evil has been exaggerated ; but if there are any girls who have been enticed into the dens, and who have taken lessons there in the new vice, that is reason enough for alarm as to the possible consequences. Vice spreads rapidly, like weeds, wherever it once gets root.

The opium joints ought, therefore, to be summarily suppressed by the vigorous enforcement of the law. If Chinamen persist in smoking opium they should be compelled to do as the opium eaters have so long done, practice their vice in private and secretly. They should be deprived of the opportunity of frequenting resorts established solely for opium smokers, and be forced, like other people, to go individually to the licensed apothecaries to buy the drug, under the ordinary legal restrictions.

(From Truth.)

ADVICE TO CLERGYMEN.

Dr. Talmage and Father Barry suggest to clergymen to take a broader view of their duties and not to rest with merely enunciating doctrines. To go ont into society to see with their own eyes what appalling vice and misery surround them, and then to battle with and overcome them. Thereby much clerical prejudice and sneer against the cloth would in time vanish.

Father Barry's persistence must eventually seal the doom of the odious Chinese dens in his parish. A day's work in ferreting out the infamous destroyers of maidens has produced more fruit than one hundred sermons and exhortations. The public to-day, irrespective of creed and nationality, feels grateful for the zeal and efficiency displayed by him. To stamp out immorality is pre-eminently the duty of those who preach the word of God. They cannot consistently shirk it. No holier task lies before them than the rescue of the young from a career of vice and misery. The growing efficiency of our slender police system furnishes also a strong incentive to practical religion. Very little reliance can be placed in the absurdly small police force. The law can be violated in their presence, and many will pretend to ignore it; and when asked to explain their remissness, these derelicts often quibble and invent excuses. *Truth* gives all honor to men like Father Barry. He has struck out boldly, right and left, from the path of his duty as a servant of God, and his success has put to shame Superintendent Jenkins and several lazy or willfully blind officers of the law.

(From the Brooklyn Eagle.)

It is a pointed satire upon the efficiency of the police in the city that the people living in the vicinity of Mott street find it necessary to band themselves together so as to protect their children from the frightfully corrupt influences of the Chinamen in that quarter. Such is the case, however. Under Father Barry the citizens have formed themselves into a protective organization and by the aid of the Society for the Suppression of Vice have waked the police up to something like a sense of their duty. The vile dens common in this locality, and the frightful immorality which has suddenly been unearthed find no parallel in any part of the city. The wonder is that a mob has not risen and swept the Chinamen into the river. The Celestials, I see, have begun to organize in the office of the *Chinese-American*, the only paper published in their language in this country, and propose to protect themselves against the authorities. Their only protection lies in flight just now. The people are very much incensed against them. It does not seem possible that within a stone's throw of two police stations such horrible practices could be carried on. There is no doubt that the Chinamen have been selling candy with opium mixed in it with such fiendish ingenuity that the children of the neighborhood have been given an insatiable longing for the drug. From the arrests that have been made, it was proved that after the little girls have been allured into the establishments of the Chinamen to satisfy their cravings for the drug which the candy inspired, they were brutally maltreated. Girls as young as 11 years, and from that up to 17, were found in great numbers, all of them showing sallow faces, glassy eyes, sunken cheeks and the lymphatic manner that characterizes the opium smoker. One of the members of the society for the protection of the children in the ward has caused the arrest of his sister in one of these dens of infamy. She is only 14 years old, but is so lost to all sense of decency and propriety that she has already been sent to the Reformatory of Juvenile Delinquents. It would seem as though it were necessary for the citizens to take the initiative when there is any important duty to be performed in New York. Else the police will do nothing.

Dr. DeWitt Talmage, always ready to make a point on the current diurnal topic, spoke vigorously upon this subject in one of his weekly talks in the Brooklyn Tabernacle, he said:

"One of the startling events of the week is the vigorous attack on the opium dens of New York, the charge led on by Father Barry and the Catholic Young Men's Association. It has long been a disgrace to San Francisco that with great opium dens, that she might have extirpated in a week, she keeps them to show to people from the Atlantic coast as evidence of the wickedness of the Chinese. Standing on the stage in one of her opera houses I said to an audience in 1880:—'Why do you not clear out these opium dens instead of showing them to us Eastern people as specimens of Mongolian depravity? You say it is impossible for the police to do it. Give me 200 armed police, backed up by as many civilians, and if you have no one else to lead them I will take the contract of breaking up all the opium dens in two weeks, and spoil your illustration of Mongolian wickedness.' I am glad that New York is not waiting for the police, but that Father Barry leads forth in the campaign of decency against filth. Bravo! Let all the newspapers and all good people support him in this movement. With their usual determination not to see iniquity, if they are paid to let it alone, members of the New York police have denied the existence of any such infamy. But the headlights of the New York newspapers have been turned on these pesthouses of sin and death, and the ignominy and outrage will be speedily hurled out of existence. What is needed in such cases is not tract, or moral suasion, or the Gospel, but police club and Tombs Court, and darkest dungeon of the penitentiary. There have been policemen in New York who have been bought up by the reigning vices of the day, and the salary they have received for the discharge of their duty by the city government in other days has been insignificant as compared with moneys they have received for neglecting their duty. Let public opinion, which is healthier and mightier as the years go by, put its anathema not only upon these iniquities, but also on the men in uniform who arrest everything but that which most needs to be arrested. It is high time that the good people of all cities rise up in their holy wrath and demand that drunkenness and uncleanness and crime of all sorts quit the city limits. I hail this week's movement as one of the healthiest signs of the times. Let all our American cities copy."

As I write these closing lines this young men's citizens' movement is still progressing hotly. I cannot foretell the outcome of it, but am glad that the general public is awakening to the hitherto horrible secrets of the new social evil. This may be the work of an organization in the throes of a sudden and unexpected spasm of special virtuous endeavor. But even if evanescent in itself, the knowledge of this vice, that threatens every man, woman and child, who seeks it through curiosity, through simple wickedness, or resorts to it after having been slowly poisoned with opium, prescribed as a remedial agent by the criminally injudicious physician, will have been through its means widely disseminated. In God's own good time the seed thus sown will produce a harvest of reformation.

CHAPTER IV.

AN AMERICAN'S PALACE JOINT.

The fact of an American deliberately investing his money in the business of propagating a body-killing, soul-destroying vice like this one of opium smoking is sufficient to evoke a feeling of disgust, and should call down the strongest condemnation from principled individuals, as it will shortly do in all probability from the courts of justice.

The pioneer in this business was Frederick D. Hughes. He began joint-keeping on a large scale in apartments adjoining the Cremorne Garden on West Thirty-second street, he being the principal of the firm who carried on the disreputable business of the former resort.

He is a devoted yachtsman, having a preference for catamarans, and of those craft he has owned and sailed the swiftest of the swift. Among the fiends he is considered a good fellow. To the entrance to his joint a short flight of stone steps led ; there was an inner glazed door and a long hall. The smoking-room was entered from the rear ; it was an extensive apartment, presenting a rich and gorgeous interior to eyes accustomed to the gloomy dens of Chinatown. The walls were covered with heavy gilt and brown paper, with tasteful dado and frieze. At either end of the room were rich mural hangings falling from the ceiling, and from the window cornices hung handsome lambrequins and heavy curtains. Two brazen chandeliers were provided with globes of colored glass, which softened the dimly-burning lights, and rested the visual organs of the smokers, while it enhanced the æsthetic beauty of their surroundings. Costly imported carpets covered the oiled floor ; they gently sank beneath the feet but returned no sound.

At the northern end of the room was a fire-place, beneath a carven, colored mantel. In the long Winter nights there glowed an anthracite coal fire, and the fuel slowly consuming seemed a not inapt simile to the physical and mental organizations of the smokers. They seemed to have no such gruesome reflections, but contented lay and gazed into its fiery recesses and imagined them to be unearthly grottoes, and conjured up a host of jolly salamanders to people them.

Reaching the length of the room on either side, and separated by a broad isle, were platforms about three feet in height. These were strewn with soft, warm and yielding Smyrna rugs. Circular inflated rubber pillows were used for the head instead of the barbarous neck-stiffening stools of Chinese origin.

In this place can, at the present writing, be found from ten to thirty habitues of a night. There lie they throughout the long dream-night of enervating intoxication. To the neophyte the toned softness of the light, the graceful abandon of the forms, negligent and lapped in lazy luxury upon their Oriental couches, the silent footsteps of the attendants as they move to and fro in the misty air, the dulcet and beautifully modulated tones in which the fiends murmur, all creep upon the mind like a vision from another world, and the imagination, reeking with the seductive fumes, yields itself up helplessly to the beatitude of the hour.

Apparently no vicious impulse, no harsh thought, no remorseful recollection, disturbs the perfect harmony of the surroundings ; and the after memory of the Circean enthralment of Emotion and Reason appals the senses at the terrible fascination of the gulf upon whose brink the opium smoker stands.

Occasionally throughout the night demand s are made for beverages either harmless or intoxicating. Seltzer lemonade appears to be a favorite with the smokers at Cremorne, but that does not preclude their indulgence in vinous, spirituous or malt liquors.

The smoking habit is claimed by its infatuated serfs to nullify the "curse o' rum." If they have no desire for it they drink it just the same, perhaps through pure "cussedness."

The joint is kept open all night and a good part of the day. Some of the most vicious fiends stay there from the opening to the closing hour, and at the last feel indisposed to leave. As is well-known, it is characteristic of the habit to hate exertion of any kind.

To one under the god *Opien's* influence time is *nil.* So long as his money holds out, he will "hang out." This joint used to be kept open all the time, but its proprietor now has the consideration to close up long enough occasionally to sweep out and ventilate his palace.

As the proprietor has truly said all classes have patronized his place; when he first opened, he was, according to his own statement, overrun with Wall street brokers, who, he says, are always after a new sensation. He once said to an inquiring visitor in whom he had confidence:

"You would be astonished if I should name over some of the people of both sexes who patronize my place. I have private rooms up stairs for the high toned ones, so that they can come and go without seeing any one but the cooks and the man at the door."

It was the night of my debut in this palace, out from which the Chinese were barred, and all there were "sovereigns in their own right"—being Americans—although their pretense of ruling themselves was a shallow and pitiable mockery. I had not smoked enough to arrive at that blissful state which cold Northern English cannot express; which warm Southern Italian comes nearer to describing with its *dolce far niente*, but which the *kief* of the Orientals comprehensively and tersely tells. It is a perfect ease of body, brain, and conscience, a carelessness for what may come. The subject knows not fear, and wants nothing. I had not reached this paradise, purchaseable for from fifty cents to a dollar, however, and lazily reclined gazing at the proprietor, who was an entertaining and companionable host.

He did not look half a bad fellow, and I reflected that he must be a lover of nature, like all Corinthian sailors; by an easily followed step of thought the host's personality gave place to Henry D. Thoreau's. My pleasant reflections upon the simple life of the hermit of Walden Pond, who was among nature's most ardent lovers, were rudely interrupted by the host's voice uttering with a laugh, the following sentiment: "Well, if I have got to send souls to hell, I am going to send lots of them." And the fiends laughed too.

CHAPTER V.

A DAY IN AN OPIUM ASYLUM.

It was upon a sunny, balmy Sabbath day, on the debatable ground between Spring and Summer, that the author journeyed through one of the most beauti-

ful, romantic, and historical suburbs of New York, to
visit the De Quincey Home, at Fort Washington. Taking the Sixth Avenue Elevated Railroad to 155th street,
I paused to gaze upon the magnificent panoramic view
obtainable from the bridge that passes by the roof of
the Atalanta Casino.   Before me was spread the valley
of the Harlem.   The river's surface was covered with
pleasure craft, steam launches, cat boats, batteaux,
shells, gigs, and eight oared barges.   Upon the grounds
of the New York Athletic Club, at Mott Haven, world-
renowned amateurs were training for "sprinting"
matches, five mile walks, putting the shot, and throwing
the hammer.   Through the colossal arches of High
Bridge the Harlem was narrowed, silvered and beanti-
fied in the perspective.   The truck gardens of the
denizens of Shanty town covered a broad expanse with
a green carpet, varied in shade by the tops of beets, po-
tatoes, onions, and cabbage.   Humble, necessary pro-
ducts of the soil, and yet in the aggregate and the
distance as beautiful as the coleus and begonia beds in
the parks.

Turning my face from the scene that strikes
the stranger within our gates as wondrous, but
which the Gothamite, sated with too many available
scenes of natural beauty, contiguous to his sphere, heeds
but little, I walked up to St. Nicholas avenue, and
wended my way northward.   After a delightful stroll
of twenty-five minutes duration, with many handsome
residences of varied architecture, surrounded by grounds
well prepared by nature to be developed by the gar-
dener's art, I arrived at the De Quincey Home.

The house had been built by a wealthy gentleman of
taste for a private residence.   Its arrangement, archi-
tectural display, and details of construction evidenced
originality upon the part of its designer.   The front of
the house was three stories, including the mansard
roof.   Elevated at a corner to a tower upon either side
were French roofed additions of two stories each.   As
the house was built upon the edge of a declivity, a

fourth basement story was gained in the rear. The asylum was designed to treat privately patients suffering from the effects of the opium, morphine, chloral, chloroform, and hasheesh habits, also for mild cases of insanity, nervous diseases, and inebriety. It was managed by Dr. H. H. Kane, who is, to the best of my knowledge and belief, better acquainted with the opium smoking habit, as it is in America, from personal experience and observation, than any other man.

Dr. Kane received me cordially when I had announced my name and mission, and was kind enough to say that he had read some of my accounts in newspapers of opium smoking with interest. He proceeded to show the house, and the magnificent views obtainable from its windows and porches. Among the interesting spots near by are James Gordon Bennett's residence, the Stewart castle, and the almost world famous historical Jumel mansion.

Dr. Kane is a young man, and a Benedict. He is energetic in his study of the deleterious effects of narcotics and stimulants, and is an interesting writer. His first expose of the subject that brought him directly *en rapport* with the intelligent public being two articles, vividly illustrated by the well known artist, John W. Alexander, in *Harper's Weekly.*

In June, 1882, he began editing *The American Journal of Stimulants and Narcotics,* a monthly magazine devoted to a scientific study of acute and chronic poisoning by alcoholic and narcotic agents.

The young physician, in dressing-gown and slippers, looked pale and overworked. He impressed me with the idea that he never could get enough work to do to satisfy his desire for it, notwithstanding the co-existing belief that he had already more then than his health gave him a right to attend to. He said that they were preparing to break up there and remove their institution to the city, which they have since done. Many M.S. prints and his library, as well as curious and note-

worthy parts of smoking lay-outs, were then irrecovera-
bly packed away.

I learned that his treatment, although it varied in
almost every case of opium smoking, was *rapid reduction*
of the quantity used. This is claimed to possess all of
the advantages, and none of the dangers incident to sudden deprivation, and avoids the indescribable long agony
of a gradual reduction. Hot, cold, shower baths and
electricity are adjuncts considered of vital importance.
Exercise, amusement and pleasant surroundings have
also their place in the sum total of the treatment.

In the doctor's book on "Opium Smoking in America and China," he describes the sufferings of victims of
the habit, which are scarce dissimilar from those who
have absorbed opium in other forms. Concerning his
treatment, I cannot do better than to quote briefly
from his book, first quoting a single paragraph from
its pages which indicates a conclusion he has arrived
at, *i. e.*, "Smokers generally do not seem to know that
like other forms of the opium habit, a single indulgence after a cure will in nine cases out of ten cause a
relapse."

Dr. Kane writes: "To one who has treated many
cases of the morphia, or opium habit, where the drug
has been used by the mouth or sub-cutaneously, the
management and speedy cure of the opium smoker
seems a very easy matter. For instance, when I first
began to investigate this subject, I picked out the
hardest case to be found among the opium smokers in
this city, a man who had ruined himself financially,
morally, and physically by the practice; one who was
looked upon by all the smokers in the East, West and
South (for he was known and had smoked almost
everywhere) as the greatest of all "opium fiends."

I offered to cure him for nothing if he would let me
try. He would scrape the bowl and eat the ash; would
steal it from the Chinamen; would pawn his wife's
clothing for opium. He was in the De Quincey Home just
four days, and under treatment but ten. He was broken

of his habit thus speedily and effectually with almost no suffering—nothing as compared to what an ordinary smoker would suffer in breaking himself. After leaving me he gained very rapidly in flesh, and is to-day free from the vice and has absolutely no craving for the drng. He had been a hard smoker from eight to ten years. Others that I have since treated have gone through in the same easy and rapid manner. I hope in a few days to be able to persuade a Chinaman, who has been smoking for the past twenty-eight years, and who is said to be the hardest smoker in the city, to let me cure him.

The first patient—the American "fiend"—had once experienced the horrors of sudden deprivation on shipboard, and did not believe, until it was proved to him, that a comparatively painless and rapid cure was possible.

This treatment consists in the use of capsicum digitalis, and cannabis Indica tincture in large doses, often repeated. The bromides of potassium and sodium, if there is much reflex nervous trouble, may be given. The bromides should be administered in 100 gr. doses, twice daily, *in plenty of water*, as then their absorption is more full and rapid. Their use, however, should be continued for only a few days at the most.

In addition to this, bismuth and catechu in large doses for the diarrhœa and vomiting; chloride of gold and soda, $\frac{1}{2}$ gr. every two hours in the form of pill or Fuller's tablets, with fluid extract gelseminum, to relieve the pains in the limbs; massage and electro massage, hot baths and cold spray for the same purpose; oxide of zinc and atropia for the profuse perspiration; and hyoscyamus and chloral to produce sleep; stimulants, of which iced champagne is the best, should be freely used for 48 *hours only*.

Later, to relieve dryness of the throat, fluid extract of jaborandi; muriate of ammonia, and benzoic acid for the bronchitis, and nitrate of silver for the pharyngitis, prove of service. Tonics, short warm baths, with cold douche or spray, phosphorous and cod liver oil, and out door exercise, are all called for. Some occupation should be engaged in that does not leave too much leisure time, and a course of reading pursued and associations cultivated that tend to elevate the mental and moral tone of the individual.

Opium smokers, like opium and morphine takers, can only be reliably and satisfactorily treated in an institution where they can be watched and restrained day and night for at least two weeks.

A longer stay, when possible, is always advisable, for then an opportunity is given for thoroughly building up the system and allowing the individual to regain moral and mental tone, without which relapse is sure to occur.

In the case of those who use the drug by the month or hypodermically, after treatment is still more important, as it is necessary to watch for and combat the return of the disease for which the drug was originally taken legitimately. The opium smoker has no such excuse of pain to drive him to his vice. He voluntarily and knowingly drifts into a habit, the undercurrent of which is sure to carry him beyond his depth and draw him down.

From the meagre statistics at hand it is impossible to say what proportion of the smokers who abandon the habit relapse.

As time passes, the memory of the agonizing struggle for freedom from the vice fades, and the former smoker, either from a morbid craving for some narcotic or stimulant, or from evil association, tries a single pipe, with the result of again firmly fixing himself in the clutches of his old enemy.

There are quacks in the West who put up medicines, which will, they claim, enable a smoker to abandon the pipe without suffering. It is a cunning bait, but a delusive one, it having led many to ruin; for, containing some preparation of opium or morphine, they often fix the victim in the double habit of smoking and taking the drug by the mouth. These rascals deserve a punishment that no law now in existence can give them.

The Chinese make two kinds of pills (both of which contain opium) that are used by some smokers to assist them in breaking the habit. Finding the number of pills that will carry him through the day comfortably, the person at once abandons the pipe, taking the pills in its stead, reducing the number of pills from day to day, until none are taken. Some few have succeeded in thus curing themselves. Others dissolve the ash or *yen ishi* in sherry wine, and take a tablespoonful three times a day, each time adding to the bottle the same quantity of pure wine. Soon the patient is only taking clear wine and finds his habit broken.

Doctor Kane had no very noteworthy cases of the "smoking" habit under his charge at the time of my visit. He had, however, one patient of such a pitiable appearance that at sight of him I could not repress a shudder. This was a Southern gentleman, once of superior intellect and culture, but then seemingly an irreparable wreck, physically and mentally. The physicians and attendants in the asylum had dubbed his the "champion" case. It was a combination of opium, morphine, and alcoholic habits.

The sufferer told me that a physician had once prescribed hypodermic injections of morphine for him to relieve him from pain and insomnia caused by a disease of the stomach. He pursued this course of treatment for some time, until it occurred to him that he might as well save himself the time, trouble and expense of medical attendance, and procuring a syringe and solution, injected the slow poison into his own arteries. Thus he laid the foundation of a monumental suffering which towered above the marks of buried happiness even among the worst punished victims of their own folly—the slaves of the opiates.

In the garden behind the house were growing some poppies with which the doctor was experimenting. In the loft of his stable lived a small colony of rabbits, all

forced by him to become slaves of habit in the name
of science.   Some were opium eaters and some received
morphine hypodermically.

Perhaps it was not to be wondered at, but it seemed
strange to know that the moment that the doctor or an
attendant entered their habitation with the well known
case of poisons, and hypodermic syringes, they should
hop hastily toward their slow destroyer in haste to feel
anew the enchantment of intoxication.   Sentiment may
be foolish in these cases. but in gazing at the pretty,
bright-eyed, harmless creatures, it seemed treacherous
and cruel for man to slowly sacrifice them with his superior power and wisdom, that he might increase those
gifts, even to save his kind.

CHAPTER VI.

CRAVINGS ON THE ROAD.

EVERY traveled opium fiend would be pretty likely to
heed as he reads the significance of the above head
line were he to run by it as fast as a Fontaine engine
could roll.   When opium smoking was a novel vice on
the North American continent, that was a dread and
real terror to the victim who had occasion to take a
long journey—the possibility that he might be stranded
in a town where there were no joints; where the local
druggists might be inflexible to his pleadings for the
drug of delight and sorrow.   At that epoch the smoker
bought his own lay-out. It is true, it did not fill the bill
to indulge in solitude in a country hotel at the risk of
being discovered and becoming an object of curiosity
and aversion to the whole reading population, should
the "local editor" of the local enterprising journal get
a clue to his secret. It at least precluded the tortures
of sudden deprivation.

At the present day, if the traveled fiends are to be
credited, and judging from information gleaned from
sporadic journalistic outbursts of discovery and denun-

ciation of the vice which has sown its seed or struck its roots in new and unexpected places, there can be scarcely a town of above ten thousand inhabitants in the United States where a sociable smoke of opium may not be had. Illustrative of this is the following story, reprinted from the leaves of *Drake's Traveler's Magazine :*

A PERIPATETIC FIEND.

A New York commercial traveler, who is a victim of the opium smoking habit, thus briefly describes a phase of this terrible and increasing social vice in the United States, of which little has been known to others than the peripatetic fiends themselves.

"I hit my first pipe in Reno, Nevada, when on a transcontinental business trip, in the Spring of 1879. There was a party of six started out one evening, which included an old-time negro minstrel, who is now a total wreck from using opium; three variety actresses, one of whom bore a growing network of scars upon her upper and nether limbs, from the use of morphine through the hypodermic syringe; a 'tender-foot' from Yale, who was going to prospect and grow long hair in the mining country, and your humble servant. The Nevada statute is the most stringent of any against smokers and those who sell opium."

"What! are there laws against opium smoking?"

"Yes, in three States—Nevada, California and New York; and I may as well admit that I ran the risk, last night, of paying $500 fine and doing three months' time in the penitentiary, by smoking in a Bowery opium joint," said the unrepenting sinner, laughing heartily.

"But, as I was saying, it was in Reno that I first hit the flute, as the fiends call the opium pipe, or *yen tsiang ;* and we had to lay low in the high grass, and sneak into one of the filthiest Chinese joints I have ever seen, because the police were so strict. Of course the risk, the mystery, and the fascination of being in odd company suggested a repetition of the indulgence, and thus

I became a fiend. I had no difficulty in gratifying my inclinations for the new-found pleasure, nor in satisfying the inexorable demands of unnatural appetite, here in the city. After my return from the Pacific slope, I stayed with the house during the dull season, and then started out again to work up the Fall trade. Occasionally I had to stay in second and third-class towns over night. At first, when I did not get a smoke for three or four days, it was only like running out of tobacco; but finally I suffered terribly. Twice I tried to buy opium or laudanum in drug stores, but the druggists would not listen to either my explanations, entreaties or arguments. One night I was stranded in New Brighton, Beaver Co., Pa. It's a queer region about there, sort of Quakerlike, because of the influence of the Economites, or Harmonists, a rich society of people who separate the sexes like the Shakers.

"There was a variety entertainment progressing in a hall on the main street, and I strolled in there, expecting to be disgusted with a snide show. But it proved better than I thought, and who should I see, as the bright particular star, but one of the girls who had accompanied us to the j int in Reno.

"It was raining—not hard, but dismally—when the red baize curtain dropped, and I stood at the door among a crowd of the young bloods of the town, who were waiting to see the 'prima donna' come out. She finally came, with her clothes gathered closely around her, and made some vexed and rather unrefined expression about the rain. I hesitated a moment, and then stepped up and proffered my escort and the shelter of my silk umbrella. She sized me up, but did not recognize me, and accepted, thinking, no doubt, that I was some flat or other.

"As we walked, I incidentally mentioned that I was from New York, which caught her right off. Then I recalled the night in Reno, and we were *en rapport* instanter, whereupon I told her of my then newly acquired habit, and its consequent cravings. She stopped

short, and said, 'why, you ain't a bit fly.' Upon
my admission that I was not fly enough to find an opium
pipe around there, she said:

"'I was going to take a smoke to-morrow morning,
but if you say the word, my covey, we'll hit the pipe
to-night.'

"I was joyfully acquiescent, and she turned to the
left, saying she had been over the route once before in
daylight We walked along a tree-bordered, wide,
silent street, and she jocularly remarked that its name
was Broadway.

"We crossed a roaring stream through a covered
bridge, which seemed dark and dismal as the haunts of
Erebus. It was a strange promenade, picking our way
along the dark and muddy road that led into the manu-
facturing village of Beaver Falls. It was but a short
distance though, and we presently turned the corner of
a great building which she said was the cutlery works,
where they employed Chinese labor. There she stopped at a door partly below the level of the street, and
softly knocked. A weazen-faced old Chinaman, with
gold rimmed spectacles, opened the door a crack, and
peered forth. She had drawn a piece of yellow paper
from her chatelaine, which fluttered in the crack as the
Chinaman cautiously took it.

"'Want smoke yen tsiang, Poppy,' said she. The
aged Mongol examined the paper, and then leered at
us, displaying his toothless gums in a horrible manner.

"'Alle litee Wun Lung, him good Chinaman, Plitts-
burg,' he said.

"We were soon comfortably bestowed on a bunk, in
a room with about twenty Chinamen. Some of them
jabbered a little about the white woman, but soon for-
got her in their devotion to the *opien* god. We staid
there till six in the morning, and smoked fifty 'Fan,'
about a hundred grains apiece or more.

"Before we left, Ah Sum gave me a piece of yellow
paper marked with Chinese characters, accompanied
with directions to present it to a Chinese laundryman

in New Castle, Lawrence county, I having told him my next destination according to my companion's instructions. She received a red paper credential to a laundryman in Youngstown, Ohio. We parted that morning after our seance with the drowsy god of the Orient, with our ties of platonic friendship firmly cemented. We have had a good many smokes together since that up in Quong War's, old Pop's in Mott street, Chin Tin's, or Jumbo's, as it is now called, under 'Paddy' Martin's Wine room on Chatham street, and at Fred Hughes' palatial joint at the Cremorne.

"Now I'm going to Newark to-morrow to stay over Sunday. There's a ticket I got from old Pop, that will let me into the good graces of a yellow fiend who keeps a laundry on Market street, if I should want to smoke, and that's the way we get it on the road.

"It's a poor town now-a-days that has not a Chinese laundry, and nearly every one has its opium lay-out. You once get the first ticket and you're booked straight through. I tell you it's a great system for the fiends who travel."

The bright, vivacious, reckless talk of the "drummer" carries the conviction that the above sketch was taken from life. To any one who may have visited the quaint and curious followers of Matthew Rapp, in their colony at Economy, Penn., the mental query must occur "How it would shock their presiding genius, the pious, and worthy Jacob Henrici, had he known of and realized, the fatal vice existing under his very venerable nose."

Brooklyn, the city of churches and of homes. There at least should be a spot free from the taint, with the new world metropolis overflowing with Parisian and Oriental vices accessible so close at hand. Brooklyn, the boast of whose police it is that there is not a brothel within its vast limits, although the "three bed hotel bill" farce has borne its bitter fruit in a plenteous production of assignation houses; Brooklyn, with its largest and most successful Chinese mission Sabbath-school,

which is converting a quarter or half-a-hundred almond
eyed Orientals to the ways and means of Christian civili-
zation, while their heathen countrymen in the vicinity
are tempting the Christain's sons into toying with the
most ominous vice of the age.

The first principle of the Chinese adventurer is to
return to China. It is doubtful whether his Christianity will stand the test on his return to old associations,
where he will again see the worship of the traditional
and historic elder religion of Buddha. But the Christian's sons will never forget their lesson. They will
continue to "hit the pipe" until they reap the wages
of their absorbing sin.

But Brooklyn has not been overlooked by the "*Opien
god*" in extending his domain, and I exhibit in evidence
the following vivid reportorial pen picture from the columns of a journal sufficiently well-known, and often
quoted, the *Brooklyn Daily Times:*

A FIEND.

CURIOUS REVELATIONS BY AN EASTERN DISTRICT OPIUM
SMOKER—HIS CONVENIENT WAY OF "HITTING THE PIPE"
WHERE HE HAS HIS COLLARS LAUNDRIED—HITHERTO UN-
WRITTEN CUSTOM OF PERIPATETIC AMERICAN VOTARIES OF
THE DROWSY GOD OF THE ORIENT.

"That man is a fiend," said a young man of extensive
acquaintance and experience, both in the Eastern District and elsewhere, on a recent warm evening to a *Times*
reporter, while both were standing at the intersection of
Broadway and Fourth street. "What, that man?"
was the astonished reply, for the second speaker knew
the young man referred to passing well, and had never
before heard any whisper of his alleged demoniac nature. "I swear he smokes opium; you know 'fiend' is
the cant term by which the smokers distinguish one of
their fraternity from the rest of the world."

By this time the subject of these remarks had drawn
near the speakers and greeted them smilingly in tones

singularly soft and gentle. The reporter scanned his face closely, impelled by the curiosity that the previous conversation had inspired. He saw nothing there indicative of the awful slavery of opium, except that his eyelids—especially the lower—were inflamed, and of a light red color.

"I was just telling him that you hit the flute occasionally, Larry," said the first speaker, laughing, and nodding toward the reporter.

"I trust he will have the kindness not to advertise it; why did you not add that you have been in the joints two or three times yourself?"

"Yes, but I shook it after satisfying my curiosity; I had no ambition to become one of the fiends," said his friend.

"It's a potent spell, and dangerous to trifle with; you may become a fiend yet," rejoined Larry.

The reporter asked for information upon the subject. The "fiend" readily acceded to his request upon his promise not to reveal his identity. It may be said, however, that he is a resident of the Eastern District, and is known to hundreds of the citizens.

"Let us board this Yates avenue car and we can smoke a cigarette and talk on the way."

"But where are you going?"

"I am going to take a smoke," laughed the fiend, and then added: "I shall begin my dissertation by saying that I contracted the habit nearly three years ago, and have had to smoke constantly since; nor do I altogether regret it, although I have my seasons of suffering. There are a great many more native American opium smokers than are dreamt of in your philosophy, I have no doubt. The characteristics of the habit in this country are different from what you may have read of them elsewhere. You have no doubt read the description of John Jasper, the Chinaman, the Lascar, and the old hag's smoking in 'The Mystery of Edwin Drood.' I have never seen anything like that and have often heard it laughed at in the joints."

"What are they?" inquired the reporter.

" Joint is the name given to an opium den. I never particularly inquired into its origin, but it formulates the idea of a convention to me, a kind of smokers' congress, because there are as a rule a number of smokers to be found in a den at the same time. An American fiend will frequently term the pipe a flute, which it just resembles when the bowl is taken off, although minus the scale of finger holes. The Chinaman for his part calls it *yen tsiang*, meaning literally 'opium pistol,' which it resembles in his eyes with the bowl attached. If the descriptions of many writers and presumptively credible statistics are true the opium pistol is doing a deadly work among the inhabitants of the Flowery Kingdom, far beyond the power of any small arm charged with villainous saltpetre. That is directly chargeable to the British empire too, but that assertion of mine opens up a field for thought and discussion too vast for interpolation here."

"How often do you smoke?" asked the reporter, breaking in upon his relation rather abruptly.

"About three times a week on an average."

" Where do you go to smoke?"

" When I first smoked in New York there was no place to smoke except in Mott, Pell or Park streets. Afterward an American woman and her two daughters opened a joint where the best class of fiends went, although the people who kept it had no character to speak of. Later still a man named Fred. Hughes opened a palatial place in Thirty-second street, West. Then Chin Tin, an enterprising Chinaman, opened a nice place at No. 41 First street. He was persecuted so much by the young hoodlums of the neighborhood that he left and is now keeping a joint in a cellar under ' Paddy' Martin's liquor store in the Bowery. Chin overtops most of the Kwang Tung men and Tartar coolies, whom you may see in Mott street, by a head and shoulders. For this reason since the advent of Barnum's pachydermatous purchase one of the female fiends christened him with the sobriquet of 'Jumbo,' which adheres as tightly as if it was stuck to him with some of his own smoking opium."

Thus the fiend rattled on until the car reached De Kalb avenue when he suddenly leaped off followed by the reporter.

After a few moments' walk the two entered a Chinese laundry, which the reporter had often seen. Before they reached it, however, his mentor said: "Do you wish to smoke?" The reporter demurred.

"All right you know; if you would smoke a few pipes I don't think you would run any risk, and Lee's suspicions would not be aroused. I have dropped on a handy resort for me here, and I don't want it broken up. Lee visits some fiends in Mott street, and they have told him about the white fiends discussing the statute against opium smoking which Senator Koch had passed last May, and with many other Chinese who have had bitter experience on the Pacific slope under the stringent laws of Nevada and California, he is growing timorous."

"Then there is a law against smoking opium in New York State?"

"Ah, yes! It was passed May 16, and by its provisions any person who smokes, sells to be smoked, or keeps a place to smoke opium is guilty of a misdemeanor, and is liable to be punished by a fine not exceeding $500, or by doing not over three months' time in the penitentiary, or by both penalties."

"Has any one ever been convicted under it?" asked the reporter.

"No. I heard a fiend remark last night, 'Pshaw! that law is a dead letter, and yet I heard not long ago that Anthony Comstock intended to raid a place at No. 17 Mott street under both that and the gambling act. At that place the Chinese are continually playing *tan* and a lottery game at which the white fiends also take a hand, but come, old fellow, will you smoke?" The reporter determined to fathom the mysteries of opium, and acquiesced.

"Correct," said the fiend cheerfully; "when you go in there with me act perfectly unconcerned, follow me into the back room, and take your hat, coat and vest off, as you will see me do."

In the laundry a Chinaman in ordinary blue blouse or jumper, and baggy trousers, and another in spotless white raiment, caught at the neck with a gold sleeve button, were ironing shirts, cuffs and collars. "Hello, Lee! How are you Yet!" exclaimed the fiend, saluting in turn the proprietor, who was in white, and the employe in blue.

"Hello, Lally. Sun velly hot," said Lee, putting down his polishing iron and shaking his own hands, as he inclined his body in a salute that was almost a salaam.

"Hello, Lally!" echoed Yet, with the child-like and bland smile, which Bret Harte christened and made world famous.

"Come on, Tom," said the fiend, as he unbuttoned his cut-away and threw it back. The reporter followed in answer to the name which the fiend had temporarily given him, but Lee suddenly stepped before the chintz curtain that hung before the doorway leading to the inner temple of the opium god.

"Who him? Lally," asked the Chinaman, sententiously, with an expression of distrust. "Oh, Tom's all right, Lee ; he's a friend of mine, and he won't split. Maybe he'll be a good customer like me." The Chinaman paused a moment in doubt, and then his yellow face gradually lengthened with a smile as he said, " all lightee." At this open sesame in "pigeon English," the fiend pushed aside the curtain and the twain entered the back room of the laundry.

It was a very dim light that pervaded the room, and it came from a smoky lamp high up on the wall, and on one of the lowest lay, with his head on a stool, a dried-up Chinaman; before him was a tray with a small lamp burning upon it. He held in his left hand a pipe with a thick stem, which was about two feet long. A pungent

but rather sweet and attractive odor, filled the apartments.   Having removed their hats, coats and vests,
and hung them up on nails in the wall, the fiend said,
addressing the recumbent Chinaman: " Loo, we want
you to cook for us."   The Chinaman grinned in a
ghastly, dazed sort of way in reply, and the fiend crawled up on another bunk, laid his neck on an uncomfortable looking stool and said to the reporter: " You
come up here and lay your head upon my breast," and
after his request had been complied with, added, " Now
are you comfortable ?"   The reporter said that if he only
had somebody to fan him he thought he felt comfortable
enough to go to sleep.

The Chinaman, bringing his tray with him, and, in
the light of his little lamp, looking like a jaundiced
spectre of evil, slowly crawled up on the same bunk.
" Say, what is he coming up here for ?" asked the reporter.   " To cook the opium for us," was the answer.
The Chinaman resumed his old posture, with his face
only separated from the reporter's by the lamp.   From
a shell upon the tray, he lifted up on the end of a long
steel instrument like a knitting-needle a bulbous mass of
something like in color, but thicker in substance than
New Orleans molasses.   He held it over the lamp and
twirled it about as a glass-blower toys with his blow-pipe.
It fused, and only by twisting it about could it be
kept from running into the flame.   As it cooked streaks
of gold were seen in it, and it gave out a pleasant
odor, which already seemed to soothe the nerves and
senses.   The Chinaman picked up the pipe, pressed,
kneaded and rolled the opium upon the bowl's broad
face, and then stabbed it with the needle, which the
fiend called a " yen hauck," the latter running through
into the small hole in the bowl.

" Smoke," said the fiend, as he seized the pipe with
trembling eagerness and pressed it to the reporter's lips.
" Keep it over the lamp and take a long, strong and
steady pull."   The reporter succeeded but poorly, and
Loo had to take the pipe away twice to clear the bowl.

The pipe was soon exhausted and Loo prepared another. The fiend inhaled the smoke in two long and several sequent short puffs and lay back on his stool with an expression of serene contentment. The next one Loo smoked himself. Perhaps this is what determined the reporter that he had had enough of the dangerous drug.

He remained, however, while the fiend smoked a dozen pipes, and developed into one of the most brilliant and entertaining conversationalists he had met for some time. When they departed, after remaining over an hour, the fiend handed Lee fifty cents.

"I should not think you would want to smoke after that Chinaman," remarked the reporter after they had made their exit.

"Oh, I don't know. One can get used to most anything. I have heard of some terrible and almost unmentionable consequences occurring from that source, but I have not suffered any myself."

"Now I'll tell you something about the guild of fiends that has never been printed to my knowledge, and I have read extensively about the opium smoking habit, as well as its use in other forms. That is, that when they are traveling about the country—and many of them, actors, drummers, yes, and public speakers do travel a great deal—they are scarcely ever at a loss to smoke. I used to carry a lay-out with me when I went out on my Summer vacation, or on an occasional business trip, but with the present system that is unnecessary.

"Now for an instance. Last Summer I went on a trip through some of the lake cities. Before I started, I went to old "Poppy" up in Mott street, told him I was going away, and that my first stop would be at Syracuse. He gave me the address of a laundry there, and some credentials which resembled an ordinary wash ticket. I smoked there one night, surrendered my ticket, got another in exchange, and the address of a laundry in Buffalo.

From there I was checked to a small regular joint

Quong's Joss presides in carven hideousness, and where his worshipper smokes the *yen tsiang*, found that he was initiating the newsboys into a vice the evil effects of which they could not comprehend, but which was, nevertheless, destined to blight their lives,

"Humpy Dan," whose figure is a familiar one about Seventh and Chestnut streets, said that he smoked when he was hungry, and it seemed to do him good. In the article the reporter seized the occasion to direct the attention of the Society for the Prevention of Cruelty to Children to the place. If they have not been sufficiently interested to inquire into the evil it is not yet too late for them to investigate, and if possible, eradicate it. While I have not much faith in the bright future of the average "newsy," some of them will retain sufficient principle, united with their quick wits, to grow up useful members of society. They certainly cannot if they contract an opium habit at their tender age.

In Chicago the evil has already assumed alarming proportions, but in few instances has it been unveiled, and its threatening dangers pointed out by the press. The traveling fiend has no trouble in entering a joint there. The Chinese keepers remember the legal restrictions which galled them while engaged in their nefarious traffic in the cities and towns of the Pacific slope only as a troubled dream. They have found the blue-coated guardians of the peace woefully ignorant and too stolidly indifferent to even report the progress of the new dissipation. American policemen, or rather policemen in America, go not beyond their special or manual instructions, and too few of them obey those to the letter.

The best known joints are at No. 74 East Van Buren Street, kept by Jim Horn, Wan Ghee's, at No. 302 State Street, Wing Lee's, at No. 342 State Street, and Quong Sing's, at No. 40 Dearborn Street. A goodly proportion of the visitors to these haunts are young men and beardless boys. The day is not far distant when the good citizens of Chicago will take cognizance of, and cry out against the evil. They will probably resort to the Illinois Legislature, get a law passed and wait in vain for the police to enforce it. In Cincinnati, Ohio, St. Louis, Mo., and at Washington, D. C., the practice is as widespread and the joints are just as accessible to the resident or the traveler. *Opien*, the god most persistently worshipped by the Chinese, is gaining more converts in this Christian land than Christian missionaries are making in China. In Mr. W. J. Moore's "The Other Side of the Opium Question," the author says that two high Chinese officials lately said to the British Minister at Peking : " Of the two evils, we would prefer to have your opium, if you will take away all your missionaries."

It would be much better for the American people if the Celestial nation would send us Buddhistic missionaries or Confucian philosophers instead of smoking opium.

CHAPTER VII.

BEHIND THE BARS.

THE irreclaimable fiend will never learn all that his self-invoked curse means until he becomes a prisoner, where the *menu* provided by the authorities does not include the solace of his soothing and necessary poison. With nothing but bare walls, and rigid and unyielding bars about him, to distract his attention from the indescribable physical and mental suffering of sudden deprivation, it requires but small pressure to disturb his mental balance, and even to make of him a raving maniac.

In April, 1882, the author visited the Tombs to see George Appo, aged 22, a native of New York. His father was Quimbo Appo, a Chinaman, and the first of his race ever convicted in the Eastern States of a capital crime. George's mother was an American of Irish extraction.

The prisoner had been charged with stealing a gold watch and chain, valued at $250, from the person of a resident of Plainfield, N. J., while the latter stood at the busy corner of Broadway and Fulton street. He was examined before Justice Solon B. Smith in the Tombs Police Court, who remanded him to the city prison until his alleged victim could be present to testify in the case.

The author crossed the prison court yard with Warden Finn, the most vigilant guardian of the prison —a savage bull dog—haunting his heels on the way, in a manner to cause him some mental disquietude.

The uniformed clerk in the corridor said, in reference to the prisoner : "He won't open his mouth, not even the reporters could get a word out of him."

This was discouraging, but a few words sotto voce and a little tact evoked a ready reply from the Chinese-American, to the surprise of the before incredulous prison officials. Appo scanned the report of his case in the *Evening Telegram* quickly, but comprehensively, and returned the clipping with the brief comment that it was imaginative, and part of it utterly false. The prisoner then admitted that he had formerly been "crooked," but had been punished for it, not alone by confinement in Clinton Prison, but by the tortures which brutal keepers had inflicted upon him while there. "Reform?" Yes, he had tried to reform. His uncle, Tom Lee, the Mott street merchant and Deputy Sheriff, had bought him an express wagon and horse, but he could not remain in that occupation because the detectives hounded him for every larceny they fancied he might have committed.

Since the time that Matt Grace and Barney Maguire opened their opium "joint" at No. 126 Crosby street until his arrest, George had been "cooking" there. With the white fiends who had centered in the new resort he became a favorite, because he was cultured, gentlemanly, and notably neat about his person.

On a Thursday evening he was cooking in the joint

as usual when the police entered and asked him to put on his coat and accompany them. He inquired for what purpose, or if there was any charge against him. They refused to say. He abandoned his lay-out and went out with them.

With a look of bitter resentment Appo then said to the author " As sure as I live I had no idea what they wanted, but I have had too many bitter experiences, and I know that if there was no charge against me it was easy to make one.

The memory of my prison days uprose like a haunting spectre before me, and I was overcome with the old fear. I darted away desperately and ran around the corner of Jersey street toward Mulberry.

The officers fired shot after shot at me, as if I had been a dog. One of them, I have since learned, stumbled and fell and the other shot himself through the hand. A crowd ran hooting and yelling after me, until at last I fell exhausted, with six or seven men on top of me. Then the officer who had shot himself caught me.

Appo's shirt sleeves were smeared and clotted with the detective's blood. The imprisoned fiend said that when arrested he was cooking for Dr. H. H. Kane. He said he had been kept in the 27th precinct police station for thirty-six hours without any food.

Learning from him that he had been a fiend for seven years, I inquired how he managed to get along so well without his pipe. " Look here," whispered the fiend, and his eyes brightened exultingly as he turned his back to the clerk. In his hand lay a number of pills of opium each the size of a large buck shot.

" So you did make your Chinese friend talk, Mr. Williams, didn't you?" remarked Warden Finn with his customary urbane smile.

The author replied in the affirmative and asked, " By the way, what has become of those other opium fiends you had here, Long and Fergoson?"

" What?" is this fellow one of those fiends too?" asked the Warden.

"Yes, he's a fiend insatiate beyond all you have ever had here," was the answer.

Between the warden's tender-heartedness and his disgust at the chronic weakness of his new boarder, his mingled look of despair and firm resolution was so serio-comic that the author, influenced most by the latter dramatic effect, laughed outright.

The warden said: "He can't get any opium in here. Now I suppose he will be howling in his cell like a raving maniac; that's the way all these 'fiends,' as you call them, do."

"He will not howl," was the author's oral assurance, with the mental reservation that he would not, until the pills were all gone.

When the latter mentioned contingency arose the prisoner howled until he had all the officers and inmates of the Tombs nearly as crazy as himself. In an incredibly short time, however, this evidence of torment was mysteriously communicated to his Chinese friends in Mott street. Through the volunteered services of a white friend a vial of tincture of opium was smuggled into Appo, despite the vigilance of the prison officials. The opium relieved him, and his miraculous and speedy restoration to a tranquil state relieved everybody in the prison.

Soon after this the prisoner was taken before Recorder Smyth in the Court of General Sessions. There he pleaded guilty to grand larceny from the person and the Court sentenced him to the State Prison for three years and six months. Appo was then escorted back to the prisoners' pen. When Court Captain Lindsay was about to handcuff him to two of the Court officers, the prisoner turned suddenly aside, drew a vial from his pocket, and nearly emptied it of its contents before he could be prevented. After a desperate struggle, which caused much excitement in the court room, the officers wrenched the vial from him, which still contained some laudanum.

The officers believed that he intended to commit suicide, and their opinion was strengthened by his attempting to throw himself under the wheels of a loaded truck on his way to the prison.

When again inside the Tombs, Dr. Hardy attempted to induce him to swallow an emetic. The patient grew furious, and struggled so that it became necessary to put a straight-jacket on him. The emetic was then forced between his teeth and down his throat, and after it had the desired effect he was walked briskly back and forth, to prevent his being overcome by the effect of the overdose he had taken of his favorite medicine.

This unfortunate young man is deserving of pity from those whom his story will horrify, as well as of blame. Through his inquiries the author learned that Quimbo Appo, his father, was at the time of his son's conviction in the State Insane Asylum. He also was a "fiend." At the time of this writing (October, 1882) he is still there " doing" a part of the seven years time for which he was sentenced to prison for the murder of John Kelly, whom he stabbed.

Quimbo Appo was first arrested in 1859, charged with murdering Mary Fletcher, a white woman, who was reputed to be his mistress. In the Court of Sessions he was tried, found guilty of murder in the first degree, and was sentenced to be hanged in July of that year. Exceptions were taken by his counsel and a new trial was granted, at which he was found guilty of manslaughter in the second degree, and was sentenced to the State Prison for five years. He served out this sentence, and in 1872 was again sentenced to five years imprisonment for the stabbing of Joseph Sinkowski.

When George was yet but a little lad, a wealthy banker became interested in him, probably because the boy was naturally bright and sharp witted, and because specimens of amalgamation of the Chinese and American natures were then rare. At all events the rich man cared for him, and provided him with a good education.

In return the protege neglected such opportunities as

did not please his capricious fancy, and betrayed his benefactor's confidence in his integrity. Finally he threw off all restraint and chose the least respectable shades of Chinese society in Mott street from which to select his associates.

While he evinced many traits of a better nature, George Appo, almost without a doubt, has had to contend in life with a vicious appetite, and a natural propensity to commit crime, his only, and terrible, paternal heritage.

The two fiends, Long and Ferguson, to whom the author has referred us being among Warden Finn's guests, were arraigned early in the Spring of 1882, in the Tombs Police Court, before Justice Solon B. Smith, being charged by Officer Schuyler F. West, of the Fourteenth Police Precinct, with the larceny of two opium pipes from Sam Sing, a well-known Chinese opium joint keeper, at No. 17 Mott street.

They gave their names as William Ferguson, aged 26 years, a steamboat engineer, then lately boarding at the Summit Hotel in the Bowery, and John B. Long, aged 19, who had lately left the Palmer House, Chicago, where he was employed as a bell-boy.

The pipe taken by Ferguson was one with a silver-mounted malacca stem, with an ivory mouth-piece, and Sam Sing, at Police Headquarters, valued it at $35. The other "flute" had a common brass mounted bamboo stem, and was valued at $10. The arresting officer stated in court that the pipes had been sold to Fred. Hughes, the American joint keeper, for a small money consideration, (which for the most part came profitably back into his hands in exchange for indulgence in opium). The accused stated—suppositiously in extenuation of the clear case of larceny against them—that they were partly under the influence of liquor, and partly afflicted by a desire to smoke more opium than they had the wherewithal to pay for.

Justice Smith—to his credit—noted that the "joint" keeper, whom the prisoners had helped to enrich, relentlessly enacted the Nemesis upon the first occasion that presented itself, because their unnatural appetite forced them to steal—and from him—to satisfy its cravings. The Court regretted that there was no law which empowered him to commit Sam Sing, and committed Ferguson in default of $1,000, and Long in default of $500 bail for trial.

When these "fiends" were in the Tombs the author visited them. The pair came lagging down from their cells on the second tier, red-eyed and melancholy. Both persistently scratched their trunks and limbs, and Ferguson, observing the turnkey eyeing him a little suspiciously, said : "You might think we were not clean, but this fearful itching is one of the torments of the damned habit." The elder of the two said that he had contracted the vice in New Orleans, three years and over before his arrest, and that he was literally a slave to it.

"He is; he's a terrible fiend," whispered the younger one to the author aside. Both then exhibited some opium pills the size of a pea, which they were compelled to substitute for the pipe habit; Ferguson said complainingly : "We've been using the ordinary gum opium of the shops for pills; it is very irritating to the stomach, which is an additional reason why we feel badly."

Concerning their accuser, the fiends said that Sam Sing was growing rich, for his den, besides being a favorite resort for the Chinese to play "tan," was the headquarters for a "skin" lottery game, wherein any amount could be invested on a draw from 5 cents to $5.00.

The author went from the prison over to the Fourteenth Precinct station. The roundsman who was temporarily at the desk was as unenlightened in regard to opium smoking as the average citizen, notwithstanding that its existence in New York was largely within the confines of that precinct.

He remarked with the self sufficiency of ignorance:

"Those places ain't dens, and there ain't many crooked people what goes there, they're mostly strangers from other places."

The two fiends were afterwards tried, and I never learned the exact result. Some time afterward, however, I was informed by a fiend that their punishment had been very slight, their terrible cravings for the drug to satisfy their self-gotten appetites being used as a successful plea for mercy from the bench.

A smoker who had once lived in New Orleans informed the author that it was no unusual thing in the city prison there to see an imprisoned fiend using his lay-out in his cell. Their friends would send in the lay-out first and hunt for bail and legal advice afterward. To this the authorities of the city prison, my informant said, made no objection.

If this be true the Crescent City can claim the unenviable distinction of being the bright Elysium of opium smoking "crooks."

CHAPTER VIII.

VICTIMS IN THE DRAMATIC PROFESSION.

Actors and actresses seem peculiarly susceptible to the secret enjoyment of the opium pipe. This may be theoretically accounted for in various ways, but it is certain that the legions of the fiends are largely recruited from the ranks of the dramatic profession, and the innocent admirers of many a footlight favorite of either sex would be seized with a holy horror could their vision pierce the recesses of the particular joint then generally patronized by the people of genius who do most delight the people at large. These mimics, freed from all restraints, are at their best while among their fellow fiends, and together with a few brilliant Bohemians they compose the aristocracy of the joints. This very quota to fiendish society, particularly in the metropolis, forms much of its fascination, and especially as all meet upon the bunks level. "..... *Equalite, Fraternite*" would well serve as a motto for the guild.

It was while chatting with a dramatic journalist in front of the Morton House one morning that a deservedly famous comic actor passed rapidly through "the square." My companion extended an invitation to imbibe a cock-tail as he came up. The comedian declined with a deprecatory shrug and a grimace, but without pausing.

"Well, you can have any thing you like, you know, from a German to a kinnica-bean-bake" called out my versatile companion.

The invited came back and said: "Now don't, deah boy, allow this extravagant spirit to overcome you. I will see you latah, but really now I haven't ah, touched yet to-day," and off he hurried again. The expression "touched" was then unknown to me, but I was already interested in the subject which fills these pages, and had a dim suspicion to what his mysterious phrase had reference.

"Smokes," said my companion, sententiously, before I could translate my askant gaze into a verbal inquiry.

I informed him that I was somewhat interested in the subject, and would like to hear from the actor's own lips where and how he contracted the habit. That night I was introduced to him after the curtain fell at the Windsor Theatre, and with my friend, the actor, and three more of the "profession," we descended into a convenient joint on the Bowery, where it was manifest that they were by no means strangers.

I had supposed that the additional members to the party had come along out of mere curiosity. It consequently astonished me a little when after sitting around on the bunks, during which the "gags," warblings and —with all due respect to the B. P. O. E.—"Rome howlings" of the "professionals" convulsed the white, and half-scared the yellow fiends in the joint, the visitors presently removed their outer garments and called for a pipe and a cook.

The subject I was interested in was shortly brought upon the *tapis* by an apparently casual remark from my friend. The actor in whom my interest had been first excited, said he had smoked opium through motives of curiosity two or three times in New York. He had afterward spent considerable time in San Francisco, and he took occasion to sourly declaim against the monotony of life there.

"You see," he said, "there's nothing to do there; you're in a city, but it's devilish dry for a stranger. You haven't got ' the square' you know, to lounge in. The ordinary occupations of eating, drinking and sleeping, grow very stale, and when somebody proposes to go low and do Chinatown, a fellow is ready and willing enough to see something out of the usual way even if it is only to be found among Patagonians. In the joints of Chinatown there was where I got stuck on opium, and it knocks whiskey clean out of time. As a rule the joints in the Chinatown of Frisco are not a circumstance to these, in the matter of space, ventilation or comfort; but the worse they were the better we liked them. When a fellow gets tired of the infernal routine of living, and wants to go low, why I've seen it in my experience that he can't get low enough."

This gifted man mortgaged his health on earth, and future happiness, because he was bored with life's monotony. The golden tide is with him now, and golden zephyrs waft him on in fortune's way, but when the tide turns, and the favoring breezes are replaced by adverse winds——. The foregoing is merely a specimen of average moralizing. Something like it passed through my mind, but it did not find utterance. The conversation meanwhile drifted off into other and brighter phases of an actor's life, and even the Chinamen laughed—at the jokes and "gags" that they could not understand—with the rest. During such seasons of hilarity as this, it would require a powerful eloquence to persuade the occupants of a joint that a fiend's lot is not a happy one.

In an interview with an actor who was subject to the tyranny of the smoking habit, he said: "I like the pipe because you can talk of it. People who take opium and morphine do it in a quiet way and enjoy it in selfish secresy. You never saw a morphine injector, or a laudanum drinker who was jolly or sociable. On the contrary, they grow morose and gloomy in proportion as their appetite increases, and like all secret appetites, it increases with tremendous rapidity, because the one who indulges in it has nothing with which to temper his indulgence. Besides, you can invite a friend to enjoy a pipe with you, but couldn't ask him into a drug store to join you in a drink of laudanum, or take him into a hallway to squirt a dose of morphine into his arm or leg."

The sufferers from the smoking habit are well known to those within, and to many without the profession. Prurient curiosity shall not be a sufficient reason to make them known here. The time must come when they cannot avoid being first condemned for fools; and then pitied by a once patronizing public for their utter helplessness in the struggle against their enemy whose conquering inroad they invited.

The author has frequently had occasion as a reporter to visit the Globe Dime Museum on the Bowery and was there several times during the exhibition of a number of Western Indians, including "Meet-me-in-the-dark," a son of Sitting Bull, these same aboriginals being afterward exhibited in Barnum, Bailey & Hutchison's tent show. Upon these occasions I perceived almost instantly upon entering the room where the human curiosities were placed, a strong and unmistakable odor of stale opium-smoke. Remarking upon this to Mr. Charles A. Bradenburg, the proprietor, the latter said that he was not familiar with the smell, but that if it did exist it must have been used by the Indians. Suspecting that they might have found a use for the drug at second hand from white men who contracted it among the Chinamen in the West, I suggested

to Mr. Bradenburg that we examine their tobacco.
Upon request of Joe Bush, the half-breed interpreter,
the Indians civilly produced two or three bead em-
broidered deer skin pouches, but there was no suggestion of opium in the tobacco, nor was there in the
flavor of the peace-pipe, which was gravely extended to
the author, who dispelled any suspicion of a race antagonism that the noble red-men might entertain
against him by taking a few whiffs.

My curiosity was still unsatisfied and I was almost
inclined to believe that there was a "joint" in the
near vicinity and subsequently made inquiries and investigation without discovering any.   Upon the occasion when the Indians came under the momentary suspicion of having added "red fiends" to the category
which already included white and yellow ones, Mr.
Bradenburg related a story about a Warmspring squaw
who had formerly been upon exhibition there.

The squaw came to the museum one morning, before
the Indians had come down from their boarding house,
having with her a strange half-breed Indian, and both
seemed to have been stimulated with fire-water to
some extent.   They intimated to the proprietor that
they were as good as the other Indians, if not better,
and to prove it proposed to parade up and down the
floor before them, as near as we could grasp the idea,
something after the style of a "cake walk" now so
fashionable in colored social circles.

Now, as it happened, Mr. Bradenburg had spent
some time in close proximity to the Western Indians,
and was aware of the venomous animosities that exist
between many of the tribes.   Although it is possible
that he secretly shares with the Honorable William
Nye the belief that the best Indian is one that has
been run over by several sections of freight and is very
dead.   Mr. Bradenburg did not desire such an invaluable advertisement as a fatal meeting between the
rival squaws and bucks would afford him.   Nor did
even the author's earnest representations that the latter

could profit, at least $10, on the space he would be
allowed for a "spread" descriptive of the gory encounter and subsequent scalp dance, induce him to
send for the copper colored lady and her amalgamated
escort, to say that he had been hasty and inhospitable
when he advised them to emerge from the museum.

During the relation of this anecdote a man was
standing near, and apparently listening with interest,
whose face was familiar, and associated with that place.
He was always around the Indians and may or may not
have been connected with their company, but the author,
to whom the man was used to nod when we met in the
museum, then supposed him to have been a hired attendant at the concern.

One evening this man beckoned to me in a secret,
mysterious way, and as though he desired not to attract
the attention of the Indians or their interpreter, whispered: "Meet me in Eisaman's, next door, I want to
give you a queer sort of a steer on the quiet."

Having imparted this mysterious request without
looking at me and scarcely moving his facial muscles he
nonchalantly strolled out.

The billiard saloon into which I followed him is as
great a resort for variety, circus, and museum people
as "the square" is for the expositors of the legitimate
drama. It was crowded with them then, but he drew
me into a secluded corner and said, impressively:

"Promise me you's wont give this away, least ways
not till the Injins have left Brad's."

"All right," I replied.

"No, but don't you forget it now; don't go puttin'
nothin' in print about it any how, not for a week; will
yous promise on the dead square now?"

I answered somewhat impatiently in the affirmative.

"An you's won't say nothin' to Brad, nor to Joe, the
half-breed."

"No, of course I won't, if I tell you so," I replied,
anxious to have the dread mystery broken to me
quickly.

" Wal, then, look here. There was a queer racket up there jest about noon to-day. I see a tall feller with sharp eyes and black hair, and a big brimmed hat, a comin' in the door an' there he stopped an' sized up the Injins. Well, they allus.say that Injins don't make no fuss when anything stirs 'em up, but I'll be danged if they didn't up there this noon. The minnit they sot eyes on him they began to 'Ugh, Ugh,' an' ' How, How,' an' raise h—l generally. Joe had his head on his arms a-restin 'em on the platform, a-takin' a snooze, an' that —oh, what's his name, that noble lookin' feller on the far end—hit Joe a devil of a crack with the pipe, an' Joe woke up an' seen 'em all lookin' at this man, an' he was grinnin'. Joe didn't an' most of the Injins didn't, but some of 'em looked pleased an' started to jump off the platform, but they got back to their chairs, when Joe told them to in ther own lingo. I took another look at this feller an' then I seen he was an Ingin too, any how a half-breed, but he was togged ont immense, looked as though he might have blown in about fifty cases for Bowery clothin' an' gent's furnishin' goods. Joe begin talkin' to him fast an' makin' motions, as if he was tryin' to coax him to do somethin', but the feller only laughed at him, an' went over an' spoke to the Injins, and shook hands all around, an' took a pull at the pipe. The Injins kept chinnin' to him same as Joe did, but he only laughed an' wouldn't have it whatever they were tryin' to give him, an' after while when they kept on he drew himself up proud an' haughty lookin' an' shook his head for ' no.' Then Joe slid up to me an' asked me to go up with the feller on a street car an' show him the boardin' ranche that the Injins hung out at, an' I did it. On the car I went to pay the fare, but the big feller had pulled out some silver an' said: 'Never mind, I've got the change,' in jest as good English as you would, an' when I left him at the board-in' place, he said: 'I'm much obliged to you,' but those are the only things he did say. Well, I thought it was blamed queer an' asked Joe about it, an' he told me

after thinkin' a little, but on the quiet. He said the
feller was the son of a chief, an' his mother was a white
woman that was stole somewhere in Colorado. When
he was a boy he came to the States and stayed a long
time, an' some preacher educated him an' counted on
his preachin' the gospel to his folks, but it 'pears he
didn't take to the preachin' business an' got runnin' off
horses an' steers instead. The white people caught him
an' was goin' to string him up, but he laid out two or
three an' got clean away. Ever since that he's been a
bad Ingin an' don't think nothin' of burnin' a settler's
house an' scalpin' the whole family. So he was a citi-
zin accordin' to what Joe says, an' and they outlawed
him, an' now his head's worth big money out in the
territories. Now I jist thought I'd give you this on the
quiet, 'cause you can make a bully story of it for the
paper, but don't you do it till the Injins go."

The author confesses to having had a momentary
vision of capturing the notorious outlaw dead or alive
by " getting the drop on him with a gun " (one of
Krupp's preferred) a la Bob Ford, and thus suddenly
springing from journalism to affluence on the blood
money which would pour in from the territorial
treasuries upon production of the sanguinary and
back-sliding hybrid theological student's body. About
this time I also became conscious that there was a
strong flavor of burnt opium in the atmosphere and
perceived that it emanated from the person and attire
of the mysterious relator. I did not charge him with
being a "fiend," but he had evidently been the means
of perfuming the heated air of the museum with the
odor which had so excited my curiosity.

When I next visited the museum the Indians were
gone, and the proprietor had gone too, on an extended
Western tour. None of the attendants could say anything about the story, and did not remember to have
seen the stranger and the sensation his entrance was
said to have produced. At this writing I do not know
whether a real live outlaw did cross two-thirds of the

continent among his enemies, with whatever motive, or
whether the story-teller was a romancer with a pen-
chant for border tales, and was but giving me the—to
him—realistic impression of an opium-dream.

"A TRAGEDIAN WHO DID NOT WISH TO BE MADE A SHOW OF."

Among the latest ventures in joint keeping in New
York is that of a man named Bessinger who opened a
resort, which proved lucrative almost from the start, in
the basement at No. 148 East Fourteenth street.   The
apartments devoted to the use of the pipe are in the
rear, and the applicant for admission now has his features scanned suspiciously by the "fly fiend" who meets
him at the door.   This is thus because the free lances
among the reporters, who are always on a keen scent
for special stories, have come to regard the fiend and
his ways as being of interest to the gen' pub', and
whenever he appears in a fresh place he gets a free but
unappreciated ad' as soon as discovered.   This righteous policy if rigorously pursued will eventuate in
smoking the smokers out and the highly moral reporter
—who is your most effectual reformer—will not abate
his perseverance so long as he gets paid for his "space."
When the shameless Mr. Bessinger began business in
his present location he drew good houses right along
from among the "profesh."   About that time there
were so many professors of histrionic art struggling in
the courts for freedom from their companions of the
other sex in art and in misery who had been joined to
them in holy matrimonial bondage, and so many luck-
less " Co.'s " had been shattered in the provincial wilds
and left their component parts to get back to " the
square" on their uppers, that an unusual number
sought to find a sweet relief in the opium smoker's
heaven.   As men about town began to "get on to" the
new joint and flocked to inspect it with the feverish
desire of the blasé New Yorker to gaze at the latest
sight or experience the last sensation, they discovered

that its proximity to the square had made it acceptable to the fiends who tread the boards. Then they went again to see whom among the actors had fallen into the clutches of "The Demon of the Orient," and perhaps with the hope of seeing also some favorite actress, whom they might easily enough approach did she exhibit no reserve beyond that required by the rules of fiendish society. For this little amusement they had to produce a fee, and the astute Mr. Bessinger sold his customers opium, and fixed an elastic admission fee for his various patrons, who came merely to look on, which was regulated only by his judgment of their liberality based ou their general appearance. Suddenly his custom began to decrease, and in a short time his best customers had left him. A fiend speaking of this place to me but a short time since said that the curious sight-seers were even steered in with much mystery and caution by interested but "dead broke" fiends who get a "divy" from the proprietor. The latter can afford to give them a very large commission because he gets the money right back in barter for pipe privileges and a shell of "dope." The result of this, said my informant, was that no gentlemanly fiend who was at all fastidious would condescend to be regularly exhibited in this style. He had then just left a tragedian in a joint near East Houston street, who had declared that it was much more convenient for him up on Fourteenth street, but grumbled, "Whatever I do I'm not going to be made a holy show of." The joint-keeper's hippodroming policy proved unprofitable in the end, and both his temper and the character of his place are the worse for it. Recently one of the most industrious, respectable, and respectful, journalists in this city went into this place with an actor, whom in charity I will not mention but who is reckoned a handsome man. The man of whom the elite lady patrons of the legitimate in all the theatres from here to "Frisco" say, "But isn't he just too sweet." This saccharine specimen began to tone up his drug vitiated system with the pipe, while my more sensible newspaper friend sat on the edge of the bunk and smoked a cigar. One of the heelers of the place came in, and after surveying the scene for a moment, walked up to the editor with a " Mose " air that would throw Frank Chanfrau's lips in the shade and asked with a diction more profane than polite, " Why in h—l don't yous smoke."

"Because I do not desire to," was the quiet response.

" Well, then, git."

"Why so?" asked the editor, with a calmer quietness.

"Look yere, cull,' said the heeler, with ferocious emphasis, "we runs this yere joint fer people ter smoke in we does, an if yous don't take a drop to yerself, I'll——"

"What?" asked the journalist, not even removing his cigar from his lips. But as the heeler rolled up his dirty shirt sleeves, one of his fellows approached and told him who his prospective victim was. The sleeves were turned down and the heeler who was not anxious for newspaper notority walked off growling like a grizzly bear beaten out of his dinner.

The gang about this vile resort is certainly tough, and Captain Clinchy should consider that his reputation is at stake with the honorable business men in that part of his precinct, until he suppresses the hangers on. The difficulty of catching smokers in the act has been proved, but he could at least rid Fourteenth street of the mob generally about the entrance.

An illustration of what people may expect was given me recently by the night manager of an uptown Mutual District Messenger office. He had paused one evening for an instant just before the entrance of this joint and was looking at something which had attracted his attention over toward the Academy of Music. Suddenly he was struck a terrible blow in the back of his head that knocked him senseless into the gutter. The gentleman was badly injured, and said that although he could not tell who did it he knew it was a man who had come from that door-way. He supposed it to be some one who was crazed with opium. Opium does not have that effect of itself, but among the associations it brings is that with professional heelers. My opinion was that the sufferer had been mistaken for some newspaper man whose fearless use of his pencil had made him the object of their hatred.

CHAPTER IX.

FETTERS STRONGER THAN STEEL.

SOMETHING has been told in previous chapters of the luxury of smoking opium. I have pictured in a mildly descriptive way the glamour that may be shed over it by artificial surroundings. I now wish that some power, for good, might inspire my pen to write in burning ineradicable letters on the minds of the readers who may be tempted to indulge in the fatal drug, the indescribable horror of it. Even the brilliant word painter, but pitiable physical wreck, Thomas DeQuincey, could not cope with the stupenduous task, but the author of these pages can at least add his quota, with the hope that the warning will save some one, if one only.

On the old world battle field of Neerwinden, where the victorous Duke de Luxembourg, Marshal of France, defeated William III of England, July 29, 1693, the following Summer the soil, fertilized by the blood of twenty thousand corpses, blossomed forth into millions of crimson poppies. The essence of millions of Oriental poppies will, if the opium traffic be not restrained, make its twenty thousand corpses in America in the years not long to come. Its slowly fatal work is doing now in China where it was inagurated by, and is still progressing, under the careful supervision of enlightened England.

Prior to arraigning Thomas DeQuincey for his base ingratitude toward the poet, Wordsworth, his material benefactor, Harriet Martineau lays a terrible responsi-

bility upon his shoulders. In her biographical sketch
of the author of "Opium Eater" and "Suspiria," she
writes: "It is to be feared that the description given
in those extraordinary "confessions" has acted more
strongly in tempting young people to seek the eight
years' pleasures he derived from laudanum, than that
of his subsequent torments in deterring them. There
was no one to present to them the consideration that
the peculiar organization of DeQuincey and his bitter
sufferings might well make a recourse to opium a different thing to him than to anybody else. The quality
of his mind, and the exhausted state of his body, enhanced to him the enjoyments which he called "divine;"
whereas there is no doubt of the miserable pain by which
men of all constitutions have to expiate an habitual indulgence in opium. Others than DeQuincey may or
may not procure the pleasures he experienced; but it is
certain that everyone must expiate his offense against
the laws of the human frame. And let it be remembered that DeQuincey's excuse is as singular as his
excess. Of the many who have emulated his enjoyment, there can hardly have been one whose stomach
had not been well-nigh destroyed by months of incessant,
cruel hunger."

The unfortunate DeQuincey illustrated in his five
weeks' record of diurnal doses for the consolation and
encouragement of opium eaters in general, what he was
pleased to term "the fact that opium may be renounced,
and without greater sufferings than an ordinary resolution may support; and by a pretty rapid (and notably
inequal graduation: Author) course of descent." How
empty though is such "consolation and encouragement" to the reader of his recorded eternal despair in
the sequel to his "confessions:" "Suspiria De Profun-
dis."

Many victims of opium, especially American fiends,
assert and appear to be infatuated with the belief that
the use of opium is an effectual cure for an alcoholic
habit. It is a sheer fallacy. The most terrible case I

have ever known or seen in New York was the breathing wreck of a man feebly fighting, with medical aid
and cheery nursing, against both habits.

A well defined comparison between the effects of
opium and alcohol cannot fail to be interesting, and
probably the best one—it matters not how often reprinted—follows :—" The difference between opium and
alcohol in their effects on body and mind is, judging
from my own experience, very great. Alcohol, pushed
to a certain extent, overthrows the balance of the faculties, and brings out some one or more into undue
prominence and activity ; and (sad, indeed), these are
most commonly our inferior and, perhaps, lowest faculties. A man who, sober, is a demi-god, is when
drunk, below even a beast. With opium (*me judice*),
it is the reverse. Opium takes a man's mind where it
finds it, and lifts it *en masse* on to a far higher platform of existence, the faculties all retaining their former
relative positions—that is, taking the mind as it is, it
intensifies and exalts all its capacities of thought and
susceptibilities of emotion. Not even this, however
extravagant as it may sound, conveys the whole truth.
Opium weakens or utterly paralyzes the lower pro-
pensities, while it invigorates and elevates the superior
faculties, both intellectual and affectional. The opium
eater is without sexual appetite—anger, envy, malice,
and the entire hell-brood claiming kin to these, seem
dead within him, or at least asleep, while gentleness,
kindness, benevolence, together with a sort of senti-
mental religionism, constitute his habitual frame of
mind. If a man has a poetical gift, opium almost irresistibly stirs it into utterance. If his vocation be to
write, it matters not how profound, how difficult, how
knotty the theme to be handled, opium imparts a before
unknown power of dealing with such a theme, and
after completing his task, a man reads his own com-
position with utter amazement at its depth, its grasp,
its beauty, and force of expression, and wonders whence
came the thoughts that stand on the page before him.

If called to speak in public, opium gives him a copious-
ness of thought, a fluency of utterance, a fruitfulness
of illustration, and a penetrating, thrilling eloquence
which often astounds and overmasters himself, not less
than it kindles, melts, and sways the audience he
addresses."

When the habitual opium smoker exceeds his limit,
and takes too large and too many "pipes," the halcyon
condition of dreamy wakefulness is apt to be passed
by for one of terrible visions.   Sometimes the smoker
under these circumstances falls into a deep sleep, in
which horrible hallucinations, disconnected or woven
with one thread into an awful imaginary experience,
become direfully realistic.

The late Fitz James O'Brien, thus described with his
gifted pen such a coherent delirium, before which the
night-mares which have affrighted the generality of
people pale.

AN INVISIBLE DEMON.

THE FANTASTIC COINAGE OF AN OPIUM SMOKER'S BRAIN.

It is, I confess, with considerable reluctance that I
approach the strange narrative which I am about to re-
late.   The events which I purpose detailing are of so
extraordinary a character that I am quite prepared to
meet with an unusual amount of incredulity and scorn.
I accept all such beforehand.

I live on a quiet street in New York. The house is in
some respects a curious one. It has enjoyed for the
last two years the reputation of being haunted.   It is
a large and stately residence, surrounded by what was
once a garden, but which is now only a green inclosure,
used for bleaching clothes.   The dry basin of what has
been a fountain, and a few fruit-trees, ragged and un-
pruned, indicate that this spot in past days was a pleasant, shady retreat, filled with fruits and flowers, and the
sweet murmur of waters.

The house is very spacious.   A hall of noble size

leads to a large spiral staircase, winding through its centre, while the various apartments are of imposing dimensions. It was built some fifteen or twenty years since by a well-known New York merchant, who, five years ago, threw the commercial world into convulsions by a stupendous bank fraud. He escaped to Europe, and died not long after of a broken heart. Almost immediately after the news of his disease reached this country and was verified, the report spread in the neighborhood that the house was haunted. Legal measures had dispossessed the widow of its former owner, and it was inhabited merely by a care-taker and his wife, placed there by the house-agent into whose hands it had passed for purposes of renting or sale. These people declared that they were troubled with unnatural noises. Doors were opened without any visible agency. The remnants of furniture scattered through the various rooms were, during the night, piled one upon the other by unknown hands. Invisible feet passed up and down the stairs in broad daylight, accompanied by the rustle of unseen silk dresses, and the gliding of viewless hands along the massive balusters. The care-taker and his wife declared they would live there no longer. The house-agent laughed, dismissed them, and put others in their place. The noises and supernatural manifestations continued. The neighborhood caught up the story, and the house remained untenanted for three years. Several persons negotiated for it; but somehow always before the bargain was closed they heard the unpleasant rumors, and declined to treat any further.

It was in this state of things that our landlady, who wished to remove further up town, conceived the bold idea of renting this house. Happening to have rather a plucky and philosophical set of boarders, she laid her scheme before us, stating candidly everything she had heard respecting the ghostly qualities of the establishment to which she wished to remove us. With the exception of two timid persons—a sea captain and a returned Californian, who immediately gave notice that they would leave—all of Mrs. Moffat's guests declared that they would accompany her in her chivalric incursion into the abode of spirits.

Of course we had no sooner established ourselves than we began to expect the ghosts. We absolutely awaited their advent with eagerness. Our dinner conversation was supernatural. One of the boarders, who had purchased Mrs. Crowe's " Night Side of Nature " for his own private delectation, was regarded as a public enemy by the entire household for not having bought twenty copies. The man led a life of supreme wretchedness while he was reading this volume. A system of espionage was established of which he was the victim. If he incautiously laid the book down an instant and left the room, it was immediately seized and read aloud to a select few. I found myself a person of immense importance, it having leaked out that I was tolerably well versed in history of supernaturalism, and had once written a story the foundation of which was a ghost. If a table or a wainscot panel happened to warp when we were assembled in the large drawing-room, there was an instant silence, and every one was prepared for an immediate clanking of chains and a spectral form.

Things were in this state when an incident took place so awful and inexplicable in its character that my reason fairly reels at the bare memory of the occurrence. It was the tenth of July. After dinner was over I repaired, with my friend Doctor Hammond, to my rooms to take our evening pipe. Independent of certain mental sympathies which existed between the doctor and myself, we were linked together by a vice— we both smoked opium. We knew each other's secret and respected it. We enjoyed together that wonderful expansion of thought, that marvelous intensifying of the perceptive faculties, that boundless feeling of existence when one seems to have points of contact with the whole universe—in short, that unimaginable spiritual bliss which I would not surrender for a throne, and which I hope you, reader, will never, never taste.

Those hours of opium happiness which the doctor and I spent together in secret were regulated with a scientific accuracy. We did not blindly smoke the drug of paradise, and leave our dreams to chance. While smoking, we carefully steered our conversation through the brightest and calmest channels of thought. We talked of the East, and endeavored to recall the magical panorama of its glowing scenery. We criticised the most sensuous poets—those who painted life ruddy with health, brimming with passion, happy in the possession of youth, and strength, and beauty. If we talked of Shakespeare's "Tempest," we lingered over Ariel, and avoided Caliban.

This skillful coloring of our train of thought produced in our subsequent visions a corresponding tone. The splendors of Arabian fairy-land dyed our dreams. Houses, walls, and streets melted like rain-clouds, and vistas of unimaginable glory stretched away before us. It was a rapturous companionship. We enjoyed the vast delight more perfectly because, even in our most ecstatic moments, we were conscious of each other's presence. Our pleasures, while individual, were still twin, vibrating and moving in musical accord.

On the evening in question, the tenth of July, the doctor and myself drifted into an unusually metaphysical mood. We prepared and lit our pipes, filled with the little bubble of opium, that, like the nut in the fairy tale, held within its narrow limits wonders beyond the reach of kings. But a strange perversity dominated the currents of our thoughts. They would now flow through the sun-lit channels into which we strove to divert them. Insensibly we yielded to the occult force that swayed us, and indulged in gloomy speculation. We had talked some time upon the proneness of the human mind to mysticism, and the almost universal love of the terrible, when Hammond suddenly said to me: "What do you consider to be the greatest element of terror?"

The question puzzled me.   That many things were terrible, I knew.   Stumbling over a corpse in the dark; beholding, as I once did, a woman floating down a deep and rapid river, with wildly lifted arms, and awful, up-turned face, uttering, as she drifted, shrieks that rent one's heart, while we, the spectators, stood frozen at a window which overhung the river at a height of sixty feet, unable to make the slightest effort to save her, but dumbly watching her last supreme agony and her disappearance.   A shattered wreck, with no life visible, encountered floating listlessly on the ocean, is a terrible object, for it suggests a huge terror, the proportions of which are veiled.   But it now struck me for the first time that there must be one great and ruling embodi-ment of fear—a King of Terrors to which all others must succumb.   To what train of circumstances would it owe its existence ?

"I confess, Hammond," I replied to my friend, "I never considered the subject before.   That there must be one.   Something more terrible than any other thing I feel.   I cannot attempt, however, even the most vague definition."

"I am somewhat like you, Harry," he answered.   "I feel my capacity to experience a terror greater than anything yet conceived by the human mind—some-thing combining in fearful and unnatural amalgama-tion hitherto supposed incompatible elements.   The calling of the voices in Brockden Brown's novel of 'Wie-land' is awful; so is the picture of the Dweller of the Threshold, in Bulwer's 'Zanoni;' but," he added, shaking his head gloomily, "there is something more horrible than these."

"Look here, Hammond," I rejoined. "let us drop this kind of talk, for Heaven's sake.   We shall suffer for it, depend upon it."

"Well, good-night, Harry.   Pleasant dreams to you."

"To you, gloomy wretch, afreets, ghouls and en-chanters."

We parted, and each sought his respective chamber. I undressed quickly and got into bed, taking with me, according to my usual custom, a book, over which I generally read myself to sleep. I opened the volume as soon as I had laid my head upon the pillow, and instantly flung it to the other side of the room. It was Goudon's "History of Monsters," a curious French work, which I had lately received from Paris, but which in the state of mind I had then reached, was anything but an agreeable companion. I resolved to go to sleep at once; so turning down my gas until nothing but a little blue point of light glimmered on the top of the tube, I composed myself to rest.

The room was in total darkness. The atom of gas that still remained alight did not illuminate a distance of three inches around the burner. I desperately drew my arms across my eyes, as if to shut out even the darkness, and tried to think of nothing. It was in vain. The themes touched on by Hammond kept obtruding themselves on my brain. I battled against them. I erected ramparts of would-be blankness of intellect to keep them out. They still crowded upon me. While I was lying still as a corpse, hoping that by a perfect physical inaction I should hasten mental repose, an awful incident occurred. A Something dropped, as it seemed, from the ceiling, upon my chest, and the next instant I felt two bony hands encircling my throat endeavoring to choke me.

I am no coward, and am possessed of considerable physical strength. The suddenness of the attack, instead of stunning me, strung every nerve to its highest tension. My body acted upon instinct before my brain had time to realize the terrors of my position. In an instant I wound two muscular arms around the creature, and squeezed it, with all the strength of despair, against my chest. In a few seconds the bony hands that had fastened on my throat loosened their hold, and I was free to breathe once more. Then commenced a struggle of awful intensity. Immersed in the most profound darkness, totally ignorant of the nature of the Thing by which I was so suddenly attacked, finding my grasp slipping every moment, by reason, it seemed to me, of the entire nakedness of my assailant, bitten with sharp teeth in the shoulder, neck and chest, having every moment to protect my throat against a pair of sinewy, agile hands, which my utmost efforts could not confine—these were a combination of circumstances to combat which required all the strength, skill and courage that I possessed.

At last, after a silent, deadly, exhausting struggle, I got my assailant under by a series of incredible efforts of strength. Once pinned, with my knee on what I made out to be its chest, I knew that I was victor. I rested for a moment to breathe. I heard the creature beneath me panting in the darkness, and felt the violent throbbing of a heart. It was apparently as exhausted as I was; that was one comfort. At this moment I remembered that I usually placed under my pillow, before going to bed, a large, yellow silk pocket hankerchief. I felt for it instantly; it was there. In a few seconds more I had, after a fashion, pinioned the creature's arms.

I now felt tolerably secure. There was nothing more to be done but to turn on the gas, and having first seen what my midnight assailant was like, arouse the household. I will confess to being actuated by a certain pride in not giving the alarm before; I wished to make the capture alone and unaided.

Never losing my hold for an instant, I slipped from the bed to the floor, dragging my captive with me. I had but a few steps to reach the gas-burner; these I made with the greatest caution, holding the creature in a grip like a vise; at last I got within arm's length of the tiny speck of blue light which told me where the gas-burner was. Quick as lightning I released my grasp with one hand, and let on the full flood of light. Then I turned to look at my captive.

I cannot even attempt to give any definition of **my**

sensations the instant after I turned on the gas. I
suppose I must have shrieked with terror, for in less
than a minute afterward my room was crowded with
the inmates of the house. I shudder now as I think of
that awful moment.

I saw nothing!

Yes: I had one arm firmly clasped round a breathing
panting, corporeal shape: my other hand gripped with
all its strength a throat as apparently fleshy as my
own; and yet, with this living substance in my grasp,
with its body pressed against my own, and in all the
bright glare of gas, I absolutely beheld nothing. Not
even an outline—a vapor.

It breathed. I felt its breath upon my cheek. It
struggled fiercely. It had hands. They clutched me.
Its skin was smooth, like my own. There it lay, pressed close up against me, solid as stone, and yet utterly
invisible.

Just then Hammond entered my room at the head
of the household. As soon as he beheld my face—which,
I suppose, must have been an awful sight to look at—
he hastened forward, crying, "Great Heavens ! Harry,
what has happened?"

"Hammond! Hammond!" I cried, "come here. Oh,
this is awful. I have been attacked in bed by something or other, which I have hold of; but I can't see
it; I can't see it!"

Hammond, doubtless struck by the horror expressed
in my countenance, made one or two steps forward with
an anxious yet puzzled expression. A very audible
titter burst from the remainder of my visitors. This
suppressed laughter made me furious. So great was
my rage against the mocking crowd that had I the
power I would have stricken them dead where they
stood.

"Hammond ! Hammond !" I cried again, despair-
ingly, "for God's sake come to me. I can hold the
Thing but a short while longer. It is overpowering
me. Help me, help me!"

"Harry," whispered Hammond, approaching me, 'you have been smoking too much opium."

"I swear to you, Hammond, that this is no vision," I answered, in the same low tone. "Don't you see how it shakes my whole frame with its struggles? If you don't believe me, convince yourself. Feel it; touch it."

Hammond advanced, and laid his hand on the spot I indicated. A wild cry of horror burst from him. He had felt it!

In a moment he had discovered somewhere in my room a long piece of cord, and was the next instant winding it and knotting it about the body of the unseen being that I clasped in my arms.

"Harry," he said, in a hoarse voice—for though he preserved his presence of mind, he was deeply agitated —"Harry, it's all safe now; you may let go if you are tired. The Thing can't move."

I was utterly exhausted, and I gladly loosed my hold. Hammond stood holding the ends of the cord that bound the Invisible, twisted around his hand, while before him, self-supporting, as it were, was a rope laced and interlaced, and stretching tightly around a vacant space.

The confusion which ensued among the guests of the house who were witnesses of this extraordinary scene between Hammond and myself—who beheld the pantomime of binding of this struggling Something— who beheld me almost sinking from physical exhaustion when my task of jailer was over—the confusion and terror that took possession of the bystanders when they saw all this was beyond description. The weaker ones fled from the apartment. The few who remained clustered near the door, and could not be induced to approach Hammond and his charge. Still incredulity broke out through their terror. They had not the courage to satisfy themselves, and yet they doubted. I gave a sign to Hammond, and both of us—conquering our fearful repugnance to touch the invisible creature—lifted it from the ground—manacled as it was, and took it to my bed. Its weight was about that of a boy of fourteen.

"Now, my friends," I said, as Hammond and myself held the creature suspended over the bed, "I can give you self-evident proof that here is a solid, ponderable body, which, nevertheless, you cannot see. Be good enough to watch the surface of the bed attentively."

The eyes of the bystanders were immediately fixed on the bed. At a given signal Hammond and I let the creature fall. There was a dull sound, as of a heavy body alighting on a soft mass. The bed creaked. A deep impression marked itself distinctly on the pillow, and on the bed itself. The crowd who witnessed this gave a low cry, and rushed from the room. Hammond and I were alone with our mystery.

We remained silent for some time, listening to the low, irregular breathing of the creature on the bed, and watching the rustle of the bed-clothes as it impotently struggled to free itself from confinement. Then Hammond spoke:

"Let us reason a little, Harry. Here is a solid body, which we touch, but which we cannot see. The fact is so unusual that it strikes us with terror. Is there no parallel, though, for such a phenomenon? Take a piece of pure glass. It is tangible and transparent. A certain chemical coarseness is all that prevents its being so entirely transparent as to be totally invisible. It is not *theoretically impossible*, mind you, to make a glass so pure and homogeneous in its atoms that the rays from the sun will pass through it as they do through the air, refracted but not reflected. We do not see the air, and yet we feel it."

"That's all very well, Hammond, but these are inanimate substances. Glass does not breathe; air does not breathe. *This* thing has a heart that palpitates— a will that moves it—lungs that play, and inspire and respire."

Hammond shook his head and was silent. We watched together, smoking many pipes, all night long by the bed-side of the unearthly being that tossed and panted until it was apparently wearied out. Then we learned by the low regular breathing that it slept.

The next morning the house was all astir. The boarders congregated on the landing outside my room, and Hammond and myself were lions. We had to an-swer a thousand questions as to the state of our ex-traordinary prisoner, for as yet not one person in the house except ourselves could be induced to set foot in the apartment. The creature was awake. This was evidenced by the convulsive manner in which the bed-clothes were moved in its efforts to escape. There was something truly terrible in beholding, as it were, these struggles for liberty which yet were invisible.

Hammond and myself had racked our brains during the long night to discover some means by which we might realize the shape and general appearance of the Enigma. As well as we could make out, by passing our hands over the creature's form, its outlines and lineaments were human. There was a mouth; a round smooth head without hair; a nose, which, however, was little elevated above the cheeks, and its hands and feet felt like those of a boy. At first we thought of placing the Being on a smooth surface and tracing its outline with chalk, as shoemakers trace the outline of a foot. This plan was given up as of no value. Such an outline would not give the slightest idea of its conform-ation.

A happy thought struck me. We would take a cast of it in plaster. This would give us the solid figure, and satisfy all our wishes. But how to do it? The movements of the creature would disturb the setting of the plastic covering, and distort the mold. Another thought. Why not give it chloroform? It had respir-atory organs—that was evident by its breathing. Once reduced to a state of insensibility, we could do with it what we would. A doctor was sent for, and after the physician had recovered from the first shock of amaze-ment he proceeded to administer the chloroform. In three minutes afterward we were enabled to remove the fetters from the creature's body, and a modeler was busily engaged in covering the invisible form with the moist clay. In five minutes more we had a mold, and before evening a rough fac-simile of the mystery. It was shaped like a man—distorted, uncouth, and horrible, but still a man. It was small, not over four feet and some inches in height, and its limbs revealed a muscular development that was unparalleled. Its face surpassed in hideousness anything I had ever seen. Gustave Dore never conceived anything so horrible. It was the physiognomy of what I should fancy a ghoul might be. It looked as if it was capable of feeding on human flesh.

Having satisfied our curiosity, and bound every one in the house to secrecy, it became a question what was to be done with our enigma? It was impossible that we should keep such a horror in the house; it was equally impossible that such an awful being should be let loose upon the world. I confess that I would have gladly voted for the creature's destruction. But who would shoulder the responsibility? Who would undertake the execution of this horrible semblance of a human being?

The most singular part of the affair was that we were entirely ignorant of what the creature habitually fed on. Everything in the way of nutriment that we could think of was placed before it, but was never touched. It was awful to stand by, day after day, and see the clothes toss, and hear the hard breathing, and know that it was dying.

Ten, twelve days, a fortnight passed, and it still lived. The pulsations of the heart, however, were daily growing fainter, and had now nearly ceased. It was evident that the creature was dying for want of sustenance. While this terrible life struggle was going on I felt miserable. I could not sleep. Horrible as the creature was, it was pitiful to think of the pangs it was suffering.

At last it died. Hammond and I found it cold and stiff one morning in the bed. The heart had ceased to beat, the lungs to inspire. We hastened to bury it in the garden It was a strange funeral, the dropping of that viewless corpse into the damp hole. The cast of its form Hammond has still.

As I am on the eve of a long journey, from which I may not return, I have drawn up this narrative of an event the most singular that has ever come to my knowledge."

In the ensuing powerful story written by J. T. Goodwin, his Godfrey Waldegrave would seem to be either a criminal or a crank. To those who can understand the hallucinations produced upon individuals of some temperaments by the opium habit, the solution of the mystery will be simple.

" I have known few men so intimately, and esteemed none more highly, than I did Godfrey Waldegrave. A community of age and tastes conduced to the intimacy, but the esteem rested solely upon the purity and loftiness of his nature. I use the word nature instead of character, because there appears to me to be a marked distinction between the terms—the one implying an inborn attribute, while the other may denote a trait that is merely acquired. The nobility of Waldegrave was an inalienable birthright. I have known men who, pricked by the spur of circumstances, could comport themselves as loftily, and whose souls could give out as pure a lustre on the touchstone of chance occasion—freakish men, whose lethargic virtue required a strong stimulus to arouse it, and only burned spasmodically, like an intermittent fever; but I never knew another than Godfrey Waldegrave in whom loftiness and purity were predominant and persistent forces, independent of all motives and surroundings, and inseparable from every action of his life.

These qualities would have distinguished him had he been only of a passive mood, content to unbonnet himself graciously to the world as it passed along. But

his nature would not permit him to play the elegant by-
stander. Amid the pageantry of that world, as it
moved before him, he saw wrongs to be righted, sufferings to be alleviated, high purposes to be achieved;
and his soul would not suffer him to rest while the accomplishment of any of these objects lay how re-
motely soever within his power.

He was a physician—an eminent and popular one—
but the practice of his profession did not afford
scope enough for the full volume of his impulse and
energies. The superfluity expended itself in a multi-
plicity of extra professional actions, some of which were
eccentric to the extreme of quixotry, but all alike, inspired by high and unsullied motives. He went soli-
tarily upon midnight missions, to do good whenever
and however it was to be done, to the extent of his
means and ability; he delivered public discourses upon
current errors and abuses, or upon themes calculated to
instruct and elevate the masses; he held at times
regular religious services, preaching a broad humani-
tarian faith designed to attract those who rebelled
against the rigor of more orthodox creeds; he over-
whelmed the press with contributions upon every con-
ceivable topic, and when the severity of some of his
articles was modified by the prudent editor, he established a periodical of his own, in which his opinions
might find unrestricted utterance.

Such force and activity imply strong personality,
and are likely to suggest its usual concomitant—egotism; but Waldegrave was singularly free from this
weakness, if I rightly apprehend it. I take egotism
to be a sickly outgrowth and manifestation of egoism
—an obnoxious excrescence upon a wholesome trunk.
A man may be superabundantly endowed with the
faculty of introspection and the consciousness of individuality, which constitute egoism in its broad sense,
and yet be destitute of that personal vanity whose tire-
som exhibition renders him an egotist. Waldegrave
possessed a greater amount of egoism than any person

I ever met. The incessant strain of his mind, the unre-
laxing nervous tension, the shock of endless encounters,
the reaction from futile endeavor, scourged him to subjective study, and made him involuntarily a lesson to
himself. The problem of his being, in which there appeared to be no possibility of an equation between the
large purposes and the small achievements, was constantly forced upon him, and in his baffled search for
the unattainable solution he gnawed his heart away,
as other scholars gnaw a book.

But this intense consciousness and study of self did
not betray him into egotistic display. He never alluded to himself out of self-love, or in a manner intended
to obtrude his personality upon the listener. Yet his
discourse was so surcharged with latent self as the un-
pivoted needle is with polarity; but he treated of his
individuality only as a known quality in the problem of
existence, an entity that served as a fulcrum for induc-
tion, a factor, a sign, a key—or what you will—a knowledge of which furnished the only clew, however un-
substantial, on which he could rely in the bewildering
maze of life's incomprehensibilities.

His vagaries won the sure reward of eccentricity.
The sneer of unpracticalness, of the inuendo of insanity,
came flippantly from men incapable of understanding
either his motives or his methods. It was this very in-
capacity, undoubtedly, that begot the scoffs.   People
are tolerant only toward what is commensurable with
their own plane and circumference. The things above
or beyond them are equally objects of scorn with the
things beneath them. If to know not what they do be
still a valid plea for pardon, these ignorant scoffers
must be forgiven, I suppose. It might be pardonable,
moreover, in one who knew Waldegrave measurably
well, yet not wholly, to have doubted the practicality
and soundness of his mind, so extraordinary were some
of his idiosyncrasies. But to me, who was as familiar
with the structure and workings of his intellect as if I
had anatomized it, he appeared the most practical and

same of men. Obliquity and straightness are merely matters of standpoint. Vary the angle of sight, and the oblique will become straight, the straight oblique. According to the laws that govern it, the boomerang goes as directly to its aim as the arrow. The ostensibly unpractical schemes of Waldegrave became entirely practical when viewed from the conditions under which he saw them ; and his apparently erratic ways, surveyed from the base of his peculiar mental organization, showed themselves to be the most straightforward of courses. It might be urged that, in weighing his sanity, this peculiarity of organization should itself be thrown into the scales. I am not of that opinion. Exceptional facts are to me as authoritative proportionately as general ones. The laws that govern the eccentric flights of comets have equal force with those that regulate the entire planetary system.

Waldegrave was not ignorant of these jeers, nor altogether insensible to them; but they provoked no resentment in him, and even the pity they inspired reverted upon himself. He grieved he had so failed in making himself understood that his purposes and actions could be thus misconstrued. But neither the sense of failure nor the certainty that every fresh effort must encounter the same scoffs could abate his zeal or cause him to deviate in the least from the course along which his enthusiasm impelled him. He had but a single object in view—to benefit his kind. His eagerness to accomplish this rendered him indifferent to all else, and he moved onward with the exalted spirit of one who cares not, so long as victory is gained, whether his own part be honor or martyrdom.

Our friendship extended through many years, during which I noticed no particular change in Waldegrave. At length, however, I could not fail to observe a difference in him. His form became wasted, his features careworn, and his ordinarily uniform demeanor gave way to spells of moody inertness and feverish activity. It was evident that his health was impaired, or that something unusual was brooding upon his mind. But he laughed at my solicitude, though with visible effort, and persistently maintained it was nothing but a slight derangement of his system from overwork. I was forced to accept the explanation. I knew he was engaged upon a work that was taxing the extreme powers of his intellect, and it was not unlikely that in prosecuting this too diligently in conjunction with his other labors he had overtasked himself.

One evening I was sitting in my study, thinking of my friend, whom I had not seen for several days, when a card was brought me bearing his name. I was surprised at this, for he was accustomed to enter without any such formality; but I was still more surprised when I read the words written in pencil underneath: "Would like an hour's interview with you if it can be *absolutely private*."

I shall never forget Waldegrave's appearance as he entered the room. The change in him was startling. His eyes were sunken, his cheeks hollow, his carriage drooping, and the old, beneficent, saintly look that once lighted up his countenance with a holy beauty, was replaced by a haggard, haunted expression befitting only the faces of the damned.

He never heeded my astonishment; he never heeded the hand I eagerly extended; he never heeded the affectionate words with which I welcomed him. Glancing anxiously about the room, he asked in a whisper:

"Are we quite alone?"

"Entirely so."

"Is there no one in the next room?"

"There is no one else on this floor."

"I must feel certain of that," he said, opening in turn the two doors leading from the study, and peering cautiously into the adjoining apartments. The scrutiny satisfied him, apparently, for he closed the doors and locked them. Then he noticed that one of the transoms was open. He shut that also, remarking that

even walls were said to have ears, and he wished to stop
as many of them as possible.

I was unable to conjecture in the remotest degree
what all these precautions meant. Nothing suggested
itself—no topic we had ever discussed, none conceiv-
able to be introduced between us—that called for pri-
vacy, much less for the absolute secrecy upon which his
whole mind seemed concentrated. As I watched him
during his inspection of the room, the stealth and intensity of his manner suddenly gave a new interpreta-
tion to his ghastly aspect. These were the symbols
of a dethroned mind, these the actions of a luna-
tic, I thought; the ignorant many were right all the
while; I alone had been deceived. The sorrow occasioned by this apparent revelation was poignant,
and I dreaded the shock about to succeed when his
words should leave a doubt of his madness no longer
tenable.

When every possible precaution had been taken
Waldegrave directed his attention to me for the first
time. The strain visible upon him until then relaxed,
his manner softened, and a helpless, pleading expression
came into his eyes. He spoke in a low tone, husky
with emotion:

"I have no right to pledge you to secrecy," he said;
"I have no right to force my horrible confession upon
you. I make it because the weight of my guilt has
become unendurable; and I make it to-day because you
have always been so indulgent to me that I believe you
will be indulgent to the last, and because I can trust
you beyond all other men."

This was not the kind of utterance I expected. The
precision of its terms and the quietness of its delivery
dispelled the supposition of insanity; but its hint of
some terrible disclosure was equally distressing. I
could conceive of nothing horrible in connection with
Waldegrave; and could I have done so no sense of moral
outrage would have been able to withstand the sympathy excited by his appearance and manner. In my

eagerness to express this feeling, I rose and extended my hand to him again, saying:

" You have not misjudged my friendship for you, Waldegrave. You may rely upon my sympathy, my secrecy, my assistance, to the utmost."

" I accept the assurance more gratefully than I ever before received anything in my life," he replied; "but withhold your hand. When you have heard what I am about to say, you will never proffer it to me again."

"Always as now, no matter what transpires," I answered, fervently, still insisting upon his taking my outstretched hand.

" Withhold it, I say," he exclaimed, shrinking back affrightedly. "Do you wish to clasp the hand of a murderer?"

" You are jesting, Waldegrave."

" Would to God I were!—would to God I were! Do I look like a jester? You have been solicitous regarding the change in me. I have deceived you basely all along. My crime was attested by every symptom you observed—by the wreck you now see.

" This results solely from overtasking your brain; this is hallucination. You know as well as I do it is one of the commonest of maladies, and have only failed to recognize it because you yourself were the sufferer."

" I repeat, would to God it were!—would to God it were! But you deceive yourself. This is no phantasm, from which I shall some day awake with a buoyant sense of relief. It is natural that in your inability or reluctance to associate me with a hideous crime you should have recourse to the common belief in my madness. I have thought of it myself. I have reckoned, in the event of justice pursuing me, how securely I could entrench myself behind it, should I choose to do so. I have even become a partial convert to it—not that any action or utterance of mine appears to me less rational now than ever, but that it seems a sort of madness, as this world goes, to think or act otherwise than

by rote. In this case, however, it is not my madness
but my trespass that speaks. The burden of secret
crime has become intolerable. I want to unbosom myself. There is more in confession than the delusive
hope and promise of absolution. It subdues the bitter
stubbornness of heart, relaxes the torturing constraint of
silence, and brings the only rest and peace a guilty conscience can ever know. Will you listen to my confession?"

"I will listen with interest to anything you see fit
to tell me, Waldegrave."

"The only motives for my crime were defiance of
what I conceived to be senseless adages, and exasper-
ation at their thoughtless reiteration. I lay particular
stress upon the latter consideration, as I believe it to
have been the chief provocation. Many a felon has let
temptation to crime pass by him unheeded at first;
but when it presented itself again and again, the recurrence became provocation impossible to withstand. Repugnance to iteration is instinctive in human nature.
The boy who wished his mother dead because he was
tired of seeing her about, the man who voted for the
banishment of Aristides because he was weary of hearing him called the Just, were not exceptionally splenetic;
they simply gave expression, albeit in a whimsical way,
to a sentiment as common to mankind as filial affection
or love of justice. Within a certain limit repetition
may be used with propriety, even with artistic effect;
but, if carried beyond the strict boundary, it becomes
an exasperating repetend, an iteration that has been
justly characterized as damnable. This is as true of
what we admire as of what we detest. Something
too much of the thing whose beauty enraptures
us to-day, and to-morrow we consign it to obliv-
ion, with the opprobrious epitaph of hackneyed
and stale. The senselessness of the whole range
of proverbial lore combined would never of itself have
driven me to crime. It might have excited disgust, but
it could hardly have aroused active defiance.

"But my passive antagonism was goaded to action by

the satisfied manner with which brainless opponents endeavored to quench argument with some trite adage, as if any vital topic could be extinguished by a stale misconception. The thing occurred and recurred until I regarded everything in the shape of a proverb with intense hatred, and sought every opportunity to discredit their assumed wisdom. A statement of the sea of bubbles I pricked by one method or another would degenerate into a mere catalogue, and be irrelevant likewise, as my course was innocent until I grappled with the saying, 'Murder will out.'

"When I first confronted it I had no purpose of putting it to test. It was offensive to me, in common with all adages; but it was not offensively thrust at me, or exasperatingly reiterated within my hearing; I was therefore content for a while with an attitude of armed neutrality toward it. But a singular circumstance rendered the maintenance of such a position impossible. As if some malign spirit of reiteration vitalized every apothegm, I was at length impelled irresistibly to repeat the adage to myself until my brain ached with the monotonous repetition. Every effort to banish it from my mind was useless ; still the clatter would run on— 'Murder will out,' 'Murder will out,' 'Murder will out.' Superstitious people would call this a premonition, or say that I was possessed by an evil spirit. You and I know it was only automatic action of the nerve centres of the brain; but by an unerring law of fatalism its consequences were the same as if it had been the boding wail of uncommitted crime, or a demoniac voice inciting me to murder.

"The self-repeating sentence assumed to me at length the aspect of an exultant challenge. It presumed upon my forbearance. In a desperate moment I resolved to disprove the arrogant assumption, and thus make a final disposition of it so far as it concerned myself. I never for an instant hesitated in my purpose after I had once determined upon it. My conscience did not interfere, either to restrain me from guilt or to plead in behalf of the innocent victim. The proceeding never presented itself to me in the light of a crime. I regarded it simply as an experiment, and thought no more of the life to be taken than I would of the life of an animal I was about to vivisect. My whole mind was bent upon gainsaying the proverb—or, in other words, committing a murder that should never be found out. I entered upon the project deliberately and methodically.

"The first point to be decided was how to do the deed. Naturally, my pursuits suggested that I should do it under the cloak of my profession, which, you are aware, could be managed easily enough; but I discarded the idea for two reasons: the experiment was personal, not professional, and should therefore be made outside of my calling; and, moreover, if the deed were done in the line of my practice, it would be indistinguishable from the common run of practitional killing—hence not a fair test case. I wanted an outright murder; not a mere professional one. The knowledge and weapons of my craft, however, entered into the plan I finally settled upon. I decided to commit the murder in some public place by injecting poison hypodermically into whatever subject I might select. This selection was a matter of serious consideration. My original impulse was to choose some one obnoxious to me, thereby rendering the killing of double utility; but such a course would introduce an element of malice into the affair, whereas I desired it to be purely experimental. Revenge should be alien to a calm, philosophic purpose. In order to prevent any bias from adulterating my motives, I determined to leave the matter of selection entirely to chance. The choice of a poison presented little trouble, as any one of a dozen or more could be made to serve. I decided upon using hydrocyanic acid, knowing that, if administered chemically pure, less than a drop would kill almost instantly, while there would be little likelihood of its odor being detected in the open air, and no possibility of a timely application of antidotes.

"When my plan was thus completely matured, I went forth to do the deed. The night was fine and the streets were thronged with people. I had thought that opportunities to perform my experiment would present themselves on any of the principal thoroughfares; but, for the first time within my recollection, the city appeared to be ablaze with light, and I seemed to be an object of universal scrutiny. I strolled about for hours with the hypodermic syringe carefully concealed in my hand, looking in vain for a chance to use it unobserved. The difficulty would not have been so great had I wished merely to kill a person and escaped detection. With only that aim in view, I could have prodded almost anyone in the thigh as I passed. But that was not all I was seeking to accomplish: I desired the cause of death and the fact of murder to escape detection as well. To insure this, I purposed injecting the poison in the scalp or chin, where the hair or beard would conceal even the slight puncture made by the instrument. Such an operation would necessitate a movement of the arm likely to attract attention on a crowded and well-lighted street.

"A man dropped his cane, and stooped just in front of me to recover it. My hand was within an inch of his head when he suddenly sprang erect. A lady bent low to examine something in a window. The sharp point of the instrument caught in her hair as she rose quickly and turned away. After these two failures, I realized that it was next to impossible to find the opportunity sought without resorting to some obscure place, or mingling in a dense crowd.

"Just then I passed the entrance to a theatre. No better chance could have presented itself, I thought. I consulted my watch; the performance would be over in a quarter of an hour. I walked along leisurely for seven minutes, then turned and walked as leisurely back. When a few paces from the entrance I loitered until I heard the tramp of the oncoming audience. I then advanced, forced myself into the thickest of it, and was borne along with the stream as it passed down the street.

"As we passed from the glare of the lamps that lighted the front of the theatre into the comparative gloom beyond, I raised my arm and carried it at a rest-breast high. A man with heavy whiskers pushed athwart me; the movement of my hand was not at all noticeable or unnatural in such a struggling crowd, and he fell upon the pavement like a clod, without uttering a sound or making a gesture. The force of the throng bore me some distance beyond him before it was discovered that some one had fallen, and a space was opened about the spot. They attempted to raise him, but he was lax and insensible. After a little confusion, he was borne into a drug store near by, and medical aid was speedily summoned.

"During the brief interval I had been intent upon two things—to discover if anybody had observed my proximity to the man when he fell or had seen the movement of my hand. and to ascertain if any odor of the prussic acid was discernible. No one had recognized me or noticed the motion. Those who witnessed the result stated solely that the man was walking along with the crowd, when he suddenly fell without any apparent cause. Evidently I had performed the operation so skillfully that no acid had been spilled, as there was not the faintest smell of it to be detected. So far all was well. After a while I pressed my way through the crowd that surrounded the drug store, and gained admittance. Two doctors, a policeman, the clerks and a few others were present. All efforts to resuscitate the man had been abandoned ; he was dead beyond any doubt, and the Coroner had been notified to take charge of the remains. I asked casually what was the trouble, and was told that a man had dropped dead coming out of the theatre.

"I stepped to the spot where the body lay a little apart, and examined it carefully. It was that of a man of about forty years of age, rather large and powerful-

ly developed by active pursuits ; features regular, expression pleasing, and general appearance that of a
sea-faring man. It was a little singular that one whose
vigorous manhood promised a ripe old age should have
drawn the solitary prize in my lottery of death.   I
turned the head carelessly, in order to see if the operation had left any trace.   None was visible; and if there
had been any, it would have been concealed by the
blood which flowed from a contusion of the temple,
matting the hair and whiskers on that side.   One of
the physicians asked if I had any particular opinion
regarding the case.   I inquired if there had been any
more noticeable symptoms when he was first called. He
said: ' None whatever ; the man was dead; the only noticeable feature was the extreme relaxation of the muscular system.'   'That was not enough,' I replied, ' to
base any definite opinion upon; it might result, as well
as death itself, from a number of causes not discovera-
ble by ordinary examination; an autopsy is the only
means of arriving at any conclusion.'   But the autopsy,
as you will have surmised, revealed nothing.

    " The man was identified as the first officer of a Brit-
ish vessel recently arrived in port.   There was no derangement of the vital organs, no traces of poison, no
marks of violence ; in short, there was absolutely nothing to account for the tragedy.   The baffled Coroner's
jury rounded off its verdict with the convenient phrase
of, ' came to his death from causes unknown ;' the remains were buried, and there apparently was an end
of it.

    " My experiment had been successfully performed. I
had committed murder—premeditated, deliberate, fla-
grant murder.   The deed had passed the authorities
unchallenged, unsuspected; and now the only evidences
of it were buried in the earth and in my own breast.
No human power could ever obtain a clue to it unless I
furnished it voluntarily—which was a precluded contingency.   Surely here was a murder that would not out.
I might exult over the proverb as it had exulted over

enced an unprofessional curiosity concerning the murdered man. Who was he that had thus unexpectedly
encountered my fatal spleen ? What aims and useful-
ness had been destroyed by my silly prejudices? What
ties had been sundered, what hearts bereaved by my
wanton inhumanity? Such were the thoughts that
drove the monotonous adage from my mind, and filled
it with an anguish compared with which the former torture was happiness.

"The first reflection of this character was aroused
when I examined the body in the drug store, and saw
what a splendid physical development I had overthrown.
Thereafter the interest in my victim became intensified
day by day. I collected all the accounts from the different journals respecting his death; I secured a trans-
cript of the testimony taken at the inquest; I visited
the ship to which he was attached, learned all that his
shipmates knew concerning him, and obtained his photograph from one of the officers ; I sought out his grave,
and made frequent pilgrimages to it; and time after
time I found myself at the scene of the murder, rehears-
ing its incidents in my imagination. The interest grew
until the dead man took complete possession of me ;
the thought of him interfered with my studies, obstruc-
ted my professional labors, intruded upon my social
life, and entered into my dreams. But the worst was
yet to come. So far the consciousness of him had only
been subjective; but at length he appeared to me as a
visible apparition, and has never since quitted my sight.
He always moves or stands just in front of me, presenting his side face temptingly for the fatal operation, as
he did the night I performed it. I know the spectre is
unreal; but that knowledge in no wise mitigates the
remorse and horror excited by it ; my mental suffering
could not be greater were I actually chained to his
corpse.

" This is what has wrought the change in me that
has attracted your attention, this is the weight that
has become unendurable. The despised adage has vin-

dicated itself; the murder is out. In asking you to respect my confidence, I have no wish to escape punishment, for anything that the law could inflict would be a relief compared with what I already suffer; but the crime may be properly expiated without entailing upon innocent parties, and upon my profession, the pain and disgrace of a public execution. Any atonement would be incomplete, however, unless when the end comes, some one should know the cause, and be able to bear witness to this additional proof that no moral law can be transgressed without bringing punishment in one shape or another. That consideration, and the uncontrollable impulse of misery to unburden itself have induced this confession.

"I thank you for your patient attention; may no painful recollection of what you have heard prove an evil requital of your kindness."

"I am more than ever satisfied that this is only hallucination, Waldegrave," I said, when he had finished speaking. "There is no material point in your statement, but is so utterly at variance with your character and disposition, that I can more readily believe the whole thing to be a delusion than that you have undergone a change which could render it in the least degree probable."

"No change was necessary to make it actually true," he replied. "You fail to distinguish between what you believe me to be and what I am. I doubt if any one ever had an entirely correct conception of another. From certain observations and experiences we idolize characters which we confer upon different persons, and esteem or dislike them accordingly; whereas, it is not likely that in a single instance the real character of the individual is anything like the one we ascribe to him. I infer from your remark that your conception of me was so exalted that it would be as possible for the leopard to change his spots or the Ethiopian his skin as for me to commit a crime, in your estimation. It was simply a misconception. There was no spots or skin to

change. The impeccability you imputed to me existed
only in your imagination; my nature really is full of
turpitude. You have judged me solely from the practices by which I have tried assiduously to overcome my
proneness to evil. They were borrowed virtues; the
native disposition all the while was the brutal one
that now comes forth and confesses to this ghastly
deed."

"Your assertions simply confirm me in my theory of
hallucination; they are as illusory as your other sta'e-
ments. But it is useless to pursue the argument in
that direction, as it would be impossible to bring it to
any determinate issue. I will take a shorter course, and
declare the alleged facts improbable and absurd in themselves; they never existed, except in your fancy."

"In that phase the question is demonstrable; it no
longer depends upon my assertion," he answered, taking
from a wallet a number of newspaper clippings and a
photograph, and placing them before me. "Here are
reports of the death and inquest; this is the likeness
of the murdered man; the killing and the spectre I
cannot show you, but they are as true as the other details."

A glance at the excerpts showed that the obvious
circumstances were substantially as Waldegrave had related them, while the picture conformed to his description of the asserted victim.

"I did not mean the facts had never occurred in
this sense," I said. "I have no doubt that a man fell
dead and was taken into the drug store, and that this
is his likeness. I meant that you never had any association with the tragedy further than being near by, perhaps, at the time of its occurrence, and possibly looking
at the remains as you have stated. The rest was the
work of a disordered imagination, which wrought out
of these simple incidents a mysterious crime in which
morbid fancy represented you to be the guilty agent."

"You admit more than you intend to. You do not
appear to perceive that the disordered imagination,

which you concede, would render me as capable of committing the crime as of simply conceiving to have committed it.   No, the murder can not be reasoned away by any theory, however plausible.   If it could my conscience would grasp at the conclusion more eagerly than does your friendship.   But the crime must remain a grim, unalterable fact, and while I live there is no escape from the guilt and remorse with which I have blackened my soul."

"Waldegrave," I said, after some reflection, " this is too serious a subject for me to maintain my part of the discussion in the unprepared way I am doing.   My inability to overcome your sophistries only confirms you in your error.   You have not shaken my belief that your participation in the man's death is pure hallucination; but I must have more tangible arguments to oppose to your assertion.   Allow me a day for thought and investigation.   I will proceed with every caution you could desire.   Will you come here again to-morrow evening, or shall I visit you?"

"If your doubt of my statement did not imply a a higher respect than I deserve," he replied, a little bitterly, " I might feel it to be offensive—were I capable of a minor sensation in my overpowering consciousness of guilt.   As it is, I feel nothing but an abject sense of having sunk so low that even my word is entitled to no credence.   I have no objection to your investigating as fully as you like, but it will result in nothing.   The secrecy I observed in executing the deed precludes any possibility of tracing or disproving the crime.   At the end of your labors you will find yourself exactly where you now are, with nothing but my word to prove that I was in any way connected with the man's death."

"Leave that to me," I said; "only promise to afford me any reasonable assistance I may ask.   Where shall we meet?"

"I cannot say, in my unsettled state of mind.   Perhaps we may never meet again.   Let chance decide

that, as it is likely henceforth to decide everything else
for me."

"Such a state of feeling is unworthy a man of your
intelligence, Waldegrave," I said, somewhat sternly.
"You know that it originates in disease. The whole
wretched fallacy has sprung from the same source.
You require treatment. Give over your labors for a
while, and put yourself under the care of some trusted
physician."

"It is not worth while discussing the matter further,"
he replied; "we should never agree. To uproot a
favorable impression of one's self is an unpleasant task
at best; but little inducement is required to forego it.
I am weak enough almost to hope I may continue to
live in your memory a better man than I am. Good-
bye!"

I extended my hand again, but he refused to take it,
and was gone before I could make any insistance or
qualify the harshness of my last remarks by more sym-
pathetic words.

Reviewing the subject in my mind, I could arrive at
no fixed conclusion, and felt myself drifting away from
the tentative one to which I had held. When I considered the purity of Waldegrave's nature, and the
humane purposes by which he had always been actuated,
together with the improbable character of the alleged
crime, his statement appeared preposterous to the last
degree, and accountable only on the theory of hallucination; but against such a conclusion stood the statement itself—calm, rational, circumstantial—the corrobo-
rative facts of the death as reported in the public
journals, and the remarkable change that had come
over him. My argument that the murder was a fiction
which his disordered imagination had wrought out of
a simple, sudden death, had been fairly met by his
suggestion that such a disordered imagination would
be as capable of committing the deed as of conceiving
to have done so. Indeed, he had overborne me at
every point of the discussion. If there was any mental

Did the act confirm his guilt, or was it only the culminating proof of his madness? The question was as debatable as the other points that had been raised by his purported confession; the deed could be urged with equal force in support of either conclusion. I finally allowed it to weigh in favor of my original convictio Patient and thorough investigation threw no additional light upon the subject; it was impossible to advance a step beyond the point at which our discussion had ended. In consequence, I naturally clung to my first prepossession, and I still believe that Godfrey Waldegrave died a victim to pure hallucination."

A blood-curdling tragedy, into which the author made personal inquiry, occurred in May, 1882, on the Yankee ship "Freeman Clark," James S. Dwight, Master, on the high seas.

It was on February 9th that the ship left Calcutta, bound for this port. Her steward and cook were Chinese, named respectively Ah Gee and Ah Cung and both were addicted to smoking opium. The story can be best told, as it was told to me, by William Williams, the first mate, and an able seaman named Francois Jean, on the deck of the "Freeman Clark," then docked at Pierrepont's stores, Brooklyn.

The mate, whose countenance and manner attested the awful impression made upon his mind and nerves on that fateful morning, said:—

"We sailed from New York for Bombay and Calcutta June 29, 1881, having our regular crew, among whom were two Chinamen. Ah Cung, the cook, had been shipped at Singapore on the previous voyage, but Ah Gee, the steward, we took on board at New York.

"They were both addicted to the habit of opium smoking, and caused us a great deal of annoyance by inattention to their duties while under the influence of the drug, though for some time we did not know how to account for their periodical attacks of drowsiness or stupidity. No notice, however, was taken of this habit on the outward voyage, but soon after we left Calcutta homeward bound, I discovered the cook lying under the long boat in the act of smoking opium. I reported this to the Captain, who came and saw it himself. He declared he would not allow the practice on board the ship, and gave orders to have the opium taken away from the Chinamen. At the same time he said he would be unwilling to take the risk of searching the room himself, and would not send another man. The Captain stayed and watched the cook, while I examined the latter's room and found, as I expected, a number of pipes and a large quantity of opium, all of which were thrown into the sea.

"On May 27th, about 5:30 o'clock, A.M., I lay in my bunk with the door leading into the mess room open, and a curtain drawn across it. I was suddenly aroused by a dull pain, and instantly realized that I had received a blow on the head with the butt of a hatchet in the hands of Ah Cung, who bent over me. While in the act of repeating the stroke with the sharp edge, I seized his arm, quick enough to change the direction of his weapon, which sank into the boards beside my head. Then I shouted for help, and continued to defend myself from the infuriated yellow devil in a half-conscious state until I was so dazed that I cannot remember what followed for some time afterward."

The French sailor related, in a mixture of French and English, that hearing the noise, he rushed half-dressed into the mate's room, and saw him struggling for life with Ah Cung, who still held the hatchet in one hand and a butcher-knife in the other. He kept muttering "Me kille you." Turning with the hope of arming himself, he was met in the doorway by Ah Gee, glaring at him with tigerish ferocity. In one hand he clutched a cleaver dripping with human blood, and in the other a revolver, the only one known to be on board was one in possession of the captain. Before any mortal wounds had here been given, all the contestants still fighting tumbled up on deck, where a bloody and desperate hand-to-hand encounter took place. The mate had succeeded in wresting the knife from Ah Cung's hand and plunged it up to the handle in Ah Gee's abdomen, making a wound from which the entrails protruded. A sailor named Johnson then felled him senseless to the deck by a powerful stroke with a capstan bar. The mate fell exhausted from loss of blood, which flowed profusely from a gash made in his hand by a knife, and a hatchet cut on the leg.

In the meantime Ah Cung had been madly chasing the second mate Lowery round and round the deck. The pursued was unarmed, and the cook savagely brandished his hatchet. Twice they entered and made the circuit of the forward cabin, the second mate fleeing for life, and the Chinaman heedlessly running the gauntlet of the sailors, who showered blows upon him as he swiftly passed. Francois Jean ran to the carpenter shop, and brought forth a keen edged adze. With this poised in the air he stood by to strike down the crazed Oriental, who was running a-muck. The exhausted second-mate, with his eyes starting from their sockets came on, and as his pursuer reached the Frenchman, the latter brought down his weapon, and severed Ah Cung's entire left cheek, which hung by a shred in a bloody mass. Even this did not stop him, and after he had dealt several blows right and left, the opium-fiend received his death-blow from a Russian sailor. He fell within a few feet of his prostrate countryman, on the main-deck near the forward cabin. The crew then repaired to the captain's cabin, and found his blood-smeared body already cold in death. They laid the corpse in his berth, rendered immediate attention to the first-mate's wounds, and then threw the dead Chinaman and his countryman, who was probably still alive but unconscious, into the sea. At sunset the following day, with simple but solemn and expressive ceremonies, the first-mate reading the burial service, the corpse of the murdered captain—who was in life proverbially a just and kind-hearted man—was committed to the deep.

It is speciously argued that opium does not stimulate its victims to crime. Aye, but deprive them of it, and its imperishable fetters bind them to a horrible destiny. The unfortunate Captain Dwight did not realize or understand the strength and kind of ties that bound his Malay-Chinese menials to their drug, or he would not thus have deliberately driven them to madness.

From an article which recently appeared in the New York *Evening Post* over the initials "M. J. K.," the following is an excerpt: "Persons of mature age occasionally become opium-smokers, but the habit, as a rule, is acquired in youth. Hence the great evil of it; for, when once fully acquired, its hold is only broken by death. It is well-known among the initiated that a physician in New York, who claims to cure victims of the opium-pipe, and has built an asylum for that purpose, has not been able to cure himself, and daily indulges in its use. Those who pretend that they have been able to relinquish the habit may be found hanging about opium places, and do not deny themselves a pipe now and then. They are simply moderate smokers for a time, and eventually fall back to an excessive use of the drug. No opium-smoker will deny the fact that the habit has ruined him, mentally and physically."

Shortly before reading the article above referred to, the author was in conversation with an intelligent white "fiend" whom he knew. This man said that Dr. Kane himself, who is doubtless identical with the physician anonymously alluded to in the above extract, was still smoking in the "joints," and that he had smoked in the same "joint" with him within a week. In this instance there seemed no *raison d'etre* for my informants stating an untruth more than the unreliability of his class.

But more because of the printed anonymous reference in a well-known journal than of his assertion, I wrote a letter to Dr. Kane upon the subject. In answer to my direct inquiry for an authoritative statement the following communication was received:

New York, Saturday, Oct., '82.

Mr. Allen S. Williams:

My Dear Sir:—Your letter addressed to Dr. Kane was received, and as he is away the greater part of the time, lately, in fact most of the time, he told me to answer all his letters ; therefore, I reply to yours.

We heard of the article in the *Post*, but did not see it. I would say in reply, that if that was meant for Doctor (and no doubt it was) it was made out of whole cloth and an infamous falsehood. When Doctor was first investigating the subject of opium-smoking, he did smoke at the "joints," and said so in his different articles, but so far as getting the habit and being unable to cure it, that is an untruth, to speak mildly. In the first place it seems strange that any one would dare say such a thing, for they have no chance of finding out anything about him, as Doctor has neither seen nor spoken to a single smoker, or as the paper says, any of the "initiated" for months. He has not been near a "joint" or anywhere where opium was smoked in (as I said before,) months.

So far as that "fiend" having smoked with Doctor at that time the article appeared it is also false He may have smoked with him, that I do not deny, but it was long ago. Doctor smoked with many "fiends" at one time, when he was studying the subject, and with a purpose.

It is a well-known fact that unless the person making the investigation smokes time and again, and see the smokers at the "joints," he never can come to the truth, for they are notorious for telling lots of things that never occur, and unless you are there to see for yourself they tell you a great deal that is false.

There was an article by an actress in a Chicago paper quite a time since, and she said that the night she was at the "joints" that Doctor was there smoking. That was also a falsehood, and Doctor replied to it; but they would not publish it as it was a direct denial.

I hope I have fully explained to you the facts, and

anything further that you would like to know I will be happy to tell you.

I would say, in closing, that the whole thing is a falsehood, and the person writing it speaks falsely. Hoping that this will remove any doubts in your mind, I remain, very truly yours,   MRS. H. H. KANE.

With all due allowance for the lesser effect attributed by progressive pathologists to smoking, than to eating opium, there are and yet will be thousands of our unfortunate countrymen upon whom these fetters, stronger than steel, will hang as heavy as they weighed upon the miserable author of "The Ancient Mariner," Samuel Taylor Coleridge, who wrote to a friend:

"*My heart, or some part* about it, seems breaking, as if a weight were suspended from it that stretches it. Such is the *bodily feeling* as far as I can express it by words." To those who would enquire as to the poet's peace of mind, the answer is in the ensuing oft-quoted paragraph from a letter to Josiah Wade, Esq., written June 26, 1814, at Bristol : " Conceive a poor miserable wretch, who for many years has been attempting to beat off pain by a constant recurrence to the vice that reproduces it. Conceive a spirit in hell employed in tracing out for others the road to that heaven from which his crimes exclude him ! In short, conceive whatever is most wretched, helpless, and hopeless, and you will form as tolerable a notion of my state as it is possible for a good man to have."

CHAPTER X.

LEGISLATION.

Except in California, Nevada, and New York, legislation restricting or prohibiting the evil of opium smoking is here untried. The matter of opium consumption as a vicious indulgence in the United States is—it cannot be sufficiently reiterated—now something enormous, and constantly increasing, the number of victims approximating half a million. Individual investigations, police reports, and unquestionable statistics have proved this proposition beyond dispute. To first control and eventually crush the vice by legal means is a desideratum with all citizens who are morally sound. The data and material at this early stage of the evil of the legal opposition to it are too meagre and difficult to collate to warrant the author in boldly suggesting how to best frame effectual laws. Therefore after a brief history of the origin of legislation upon this subject in the Empire state it will be well to note the comments of that most heeded censor of public morals, the PRESS.

From time to time, during several years past, the New York journals have assigned their reporters to "work up" the curiosities of existence in Chinatown, the opium dens being included, and it was a regular part of the business to invest them with more or less romance and mystery. These attributes were provided by the ready pen of the reporter—it often becomes a magic wand when he has the latitude afforded by a special story—the first because it intensified the interest to the reader; the second because the dens were in reality a sealed mystery to the merely inquisitive visitor, in so far as the cunning and secretive Chinamen could make them so.

When Dr. Kane became interested in the subject he became ostensibly a fiend himself. His most fair unveiling of the new social evil late in 1881, in *Harper's Weekly*, had its interest enhanced by the accompanying sketches from life by the master hand of the young American artist, Alexander.

About the last of January, 1882, an article that attracted considerable attention to the subject appeared in *Truth*. In its issue of February 12, 1882, the *Sun* published a lengthy article in its news columns written in a style worthy of Dickens. The scribes who wrote these accounts penetrated into almost every "joint" of note in the city, but unlike their many predecessors they were piloted by fiends. Without the guiding care of their respective Virgils, the descriptive abilities of these Dantes would have been of little use. As the latter had been previously, carefully coached upon the ethics of the joints, they enacted the role of Fiend so successfully that their real character was never questioned, if indeed any suspicions whatever were aroused among the smokers or joint-keepers. Thereafter nearly all of the daily papers investigated the subject specifically, or as occurrences in the dens suggested.

On February 8, 1882, Senator Koch introduced into the Assembly at Albany, the following Bill, which, on May 16th, became a law:

"SECTION 1.—Every person who opens or maintains, to be resorted to by other persons, any place where opium or any of its preparations is sold or given away to be smoked at such place, and any person who at such place sells or gives away any opium, or its said preparations, to be there smoked or otherwise used, and any person who visits or resorts to any such place for the purpose of smoking opium or its said preparations, shall be deemed guilty of a misdemeanor, and upon conviction thereof shall be punished by a fine not exceeding $500, or by imprisonment in the penitentiary not exceeding three months, or by both such fine and imprisonment

SECTION 2.—This act shall take effect immediately."

The above is substantially a copy of the act placed on the statute book in California in 1881.

The next day *Truth* editorially suggested and with obvious pertinence, that the bill was defective as offered and asserted that such a law would not suppress the traffic, continuing:

"In the first place, to make the visitor equally guilty with the proprietor of the den is to prevent all possibility of getting evidence, and to discredit whatever evidence might be got. A distinction should be made between the visitor who goes by proper authority for the purpose of procuring evidence and the one who goes solely to gratify his appetite, and in the case of the latter an inducement to expose the dens should be held out by some provision remitting any penalty which he might have incurred, and giving him a moiety of the fine in consideration of his information furnished to the authorities.

And the punishment proposed for the proprietors of these dens is altogether too light. It might be sufficient if an amendment were made making a second offence felony, punishable upon conviction with imprisonment in the State Prison."

The *Herald* said:

"Before condemning the severe bill for the prohibition of opium smoking which Senator Koch introduced at Albany yesterday we would like to know its provisions in detail ; but surely the abstract of it which is telegraphed looks unduly censorious of one form of drunkenness in comparison with others. If there is danger of a considerable part of the people of New York fuddling their brains with the fumes of opium, perhaps it may be justifiable to punish the opium seller and the opium smoker, each with three months imprisonment and five hundred dollars fine for every single offence, as Mr. Koch is reported to propose. At any rate, we will not say it is not so till we hear Mr. Koch's argument. But how would Mr. Koch greet an amendment applying the same penalty to both seller and consumer in all other cases of drunkenness—as, for example, drunkenness induced by spirituous or malt liquors ? Can Mr. Koch make a defensible discrimination that will justify his desire to regulate personal habits in the use of opium and at the same time will not justify some other fanatic's desire to regulate personal habits in the use of beer or champagne ? We are open to be instructed by Mr. Koch concerning the perniciousness of intoxication by opium, relatively to other methods of the vice; but so far as we at present understand the subject, the opium drunkard in his intercourse with the community (which we presume is the theory on which Mr. Koch proposes to control his habits,) is not nearly so dangerous as malt or spirituous drunkards are. At any rate we never have heard of an instance of any opium smoker in his highest pitch of exaltation, shooting or stabbing his wife, or braining his child with a poker.

The *Graphic*, in the same issue in which appeared a full-page cartoon entitled "At the Root of the Question," wherein the Genius of Manhattan Island, in Knickerbocker costume, was depicted as clutching a Chinaman by the queue, who was carrying a package of opium, bearing a British label, into a joint, made the following editorial comment:

"If those who claim to have made the opium smoking habit a subject of special study are to be believed in all they say, then this energetic, ever-active, American nation is being rapidly converted into a dreamy, inane, neither dead nor alive sort of race, which, in course of time, will display all the bad qualities of the Chinese and none of their good ones. Opium smoking dens, we are told, are to be found in nearly every city in the Union, and people of respectability as well as the most depraved characters are reported to frequent them. Commercial travelers, especially, are said to be taking to the vice in large numbers, and as each *habitue* of the opium den takes great pride in making converts, the work of proselyting is going on very actively. In California and Nevada, and possibly some other States, the selling and the smoking of the drug have both been made criminal offences, but instead of suppressing the traffic or the habit, these laws seem only to have added an additional zest to the devotees of the latter, at least. In San Francisco the dens in the Chinese quarter, to which white men resorted formerly, have nearly all been closed up, it is true, in so far as the police know, but smoking has by no means been suppressed. It is only being indulged in in the better parts of the city, where police interference is less to be feared. The sumptuary laws have only had the effect of bringing the habit into closer contact with the every-day life of respectable society, just as Maine laws in many cases transferred drinking habits from the village tavern to the home circle. Opium smoking is an evil and a great one, and the question of abating it should be seriously considered."

A law making the sale of it by any one but a regularly licensed pharmacist on a physician's prescription a police offence may do some good, but not much, and to punish the smokers themselves, experience has shown, is only likely to increase their number by adding the charm of forbidden fruit to it. The best way of dealing with the question, perhaps, would be to impose such a rate of duty on opium imported into the country as would practically take it out of the reach of any but the very wealthy. Such a duty would bear hard on the poor, who need it for purely legitimate medicinal purposes, but in legislation of this sort there is always a choice of evils.

When *Harper's Weekly* published an illustrated article descriptive of an "opium smoking saloon" in China, on December 11th, 1858, its editors could not have foreseen that they or their successors would in 1881–'82 have devoted columns of space to the existing and growing evil in the city of their publication. Among their utterances upon the subject, the following is quoted:

"The first movement of any importance against the keepers of opium dens in this city was made a short time ago upon the complaint of persons who were annoyed by the frequenters of the dens near their homes. The police found that although a law against keeping such resorts had been enacted some three months previously, they had not received official notification that it was in force, and they were compelled to raid the dens simply as disorderly places. Backed by the support of wealthy Chinamen and by their own resources—which in some instances are considerable—the keepers of the dens show a disposition to give the authorities a tussle b fore yielding. It has been suggested that if other methods of procedure should prove ineffectual, the

opium-den keepers could be prosecuted under a law
governing the sale of poisons, which provides that no
persons who are not graduates in medicine, or have not
been apprenticed during two years to a chemist, shall
retail poisonous drugs. The penalty for violation of
this law is a fine of one hundred dollars, or imprisonment for six months. In proceeding against the opium
dens, the authorities have, as is usual, attacked first the
weakest and those least productive of harm, and there
seems to be ground for the fear that their zeal will have
been spent before the big and harmful "joints" in the
upper part of the city are reached "

On the suggestion that the clause, making it a misdemeanor for any person to visit an opium den for the
purpose of smoking the drug, was unconstitutional, and
could not be enforced—as a person buying liquor on
Sunday cannot be punished, though it is against the law
to sell liquor on Sunday, and the seller is liable to arrest—a New York *World* reporter interviewed Assis-
tant District-Attorney Fellows.

Colonel Fellows said: "I do not see that the law is
in any respect unconstitutional. The Legislature has
a right to pass as many sumptuary laws as it pleases.
The act is like the Maine Liquor Law, under which
one may be arrested for buying liquor. The idea
is that by making the very use of the drug illegal, the
user becomes amenable to the law. The sale of liquor
is not absolutely prohibited; it is only on certain days
that its sale is not allowed; consequently, the law does
not regard the buyer of liquor as an offender. But this
law declares that all use of opium, at least as an indulgence, is illegal—it is contrary to public policy to use
it; therefore the buyer is as guilty as the seller."

Superintendent of Police Walling was quoted as un-
hesitatingly expressing his opinion that the law was
unconstitutional. He said: "It is all right to close up
the dens; that ought to be done; but I do not believe
that the Legislature has a right to prohibit a man's
using any article he pleases to use so long as he does

not make a public nuisance of himself. You may get as drunk as you want in your own house, and if you do not annoy others the law cannot interfere."

In this opinion Colonel Charles Spencer, and two other legal gentlemen there present, coincided. Colonel Fellows added, however, that a man had not an inherent right to get drunk in his own house, and that such a right would not exist if the Legislature should declare the use of liquor illegal.

The *Police Gazette* illustrated the effect of opium smoking in a sensational way, with a full-page cut ludicrously exaggerated, but the accompanying comment was truer, although it will well bear the proverbial seasoning of a grain of salt before acceptance. "The frightful results of the opium habit were startlingly illustrated in a scene our artist encountered in Mott street last week.

"In front of one of the Chinese opium dens two young women, who had been indulging in the demoralizing pleasures of the pipe until they had lost control of their nerves, were rendering themselves objects of derision for a motley rabble of the lowest order. A policeman opportunely removed the victims of the debasing vice to the station house, where they were left to sleep off the effects of their debauch, and pay a fine for the privilege in the morning. It is a significant commentary on the alarming spread of this species of dissipation, that such scenes as the one we picture are by no means uncommon, and that the slums in which the "opium joints" are located are constantly becoming better acquainted with them."

These journalistic and official utterances are invested with interest for all those who may be solicitous for the righteous result of a moral and legal contest with the new vice in their own commonwealth, and the record may be useful to the people of other States where it is only a question of time that the subject will have to be similarly considered.

Early in March, 1883, Police Captain Alexander S.

Williams, of the Twenty-ninth Precinct, raided an opium joint at No. 104 West Twenty-sixth street, arresting the proprietor, Ah Hing, and Edward Tennis, of No. 253 East Forty-second street. The police also seized seven lay-outs, and a small quantity of opium. After a night in the station-house, both prisoners were committed in default of $500 bail in the Jefferson Market Police Court.

Their case came up the next day in the Court of Special Sessions before Justices Kilbreth, Smith and Ford. The Mongolian and Cancasian fiends looked miserable and dejected as they leaned against the bar and gazed at their counsel and the tribunal which was to decide their fate. Captain Williams rested his tall form against a rail beside the reporters' table, where sat the author, and an officer stood near him holding a bag containing the paraphernalia of Ah Hing's profession, and his stock in trade.

The prisoners' counsel moved for a dismissal, on the ground that the complaint did not allege that the prisoners had been caught smoking—notwithstanding the circumstantial evidence contained in every inch of their surroundings—and that therefore the charge was but a conclusion of facts, also that while one was ostensibly the proprietor and the other a patron, both were charged with keeping a joint. The Court laid its triple head together for a half-hour, and pored over various legal authorities. The author asked Captain Williams if he was aware that it was the first case of an arrest based upon the statute of May 16th, 1882.

He said, " Yes, and I am determined to root the vice out of my precinct if the courts will only convict the law-breakers. If there is any one particular form of vice that I am down on, it is this opium-smoking, because I have been watching its progress with deep interest, and I know it, in the end, fosters all other vices."

Justice Kilbreth finally remanded the prisoners into Captain Williams' custody until he made another charge against them.

The Captain with a smile whispered to the writer, " I always kick up a fuss, or meet with delay and difficulty somehow when I get into court; I don't know how it is," and he marched his prisoners out and over to Jefferson Market Court.

They were back in less than an hour, and the author waited to see the first effect of a law that he had helped to make. The police were not to be encouraged by a conviction, however. The prisoners were discharged for lack of evidence, and the pipes, lamps, trays, and opium were ordered to be returned to Ah Hing, who departed with a high opinion of his Caucasian judges. Thus in the first instance of the invocation of this law, it was shown that it will be next to impossible to catch the fiends in the act of smoking, and that the law will be inoperative unless it is amended so as to remit any penalty that an informer might incur in procuring evidence, and to reward him with a moiety of the fine.

The preservation of the health, minds and morals of our people against this insidious enemy is within the power of Congress. In January, 1883, a bill providing that no Chinese subject shall import opium into the United States, and no citizen of the United States shall import opium into China, was introduced, but was not passed, although it was favorably reported by the Committee on Foreign Relations, of which Senator Windom was chairman. Of course this only affected the Chinaman, and the American was left to monopolize the importing of what has become a profitable article of trade for which there is a great and growing demand. Any restriction, however slight, is a step in the right path, and it is to be regretted that the bill which provided as a penalty, forfeiture of the article, $500 fine, and imprisonment for six months did not become a law.

There is no excuse for the importation of smoking opium. It is not the officinal extract, and the physicians and apothecaries have no need of it. Let Congress, then, not restrict its ingress by heavy duties, thus recognizing it as an article of legitimate commerce, but prohibit it by penalties which the most daring smuggler will not brave.

The legions of persevering men, and brave and patient women who are battling under different mottoes, according to their light, in the name of Temperance throughout this land against Alcohol, will yet have to make of opium an open enemy. The spirit of alcohol is active and rampant. Its advocates are combining for strength, and are defiant, but the opium demon lies passive in his den, and the quieter he is, the greater will be his conquests. Let Congress stop the supply by cast-iron stipulations in her Chinese treaties, and by laws preventing the landing of opium for smoking. Then root out the joint-keepers; stop their nefarious business by local legislation, and cure the twenty thousand miserable victims already in the toils—if you can.

CHAPTER XI.

DEATH AT THE MORGUE.

The author, one bright sunny afternoon, paid a visit to the morgue at the foot of East Twenty-sixth street. The keeper, Mr. Albert N. White, was selecting a pine coffin from among a stack of one hundred or so. He said they had the body of a Chinaman there who had died from the effects of smoking opium.

I was curious about the first case of the kind that had then come under my observation, and followed him into the morgue proper, with its slabs bearing ghastly burdens, and its hideous gallery of photographs of the unknown dead. From there he led me through the post-mortem room, where upon the operating slabs were more horrors, across a paved courtyard and into the dead-house.

The latter is a long, low shed, which is built upon piles, and extends far out over the water. There were a dozen plain pine coffins within of various sizes. They were roughly shaped and not joined with particular neatness. The morgue-keeper ran his eye along the unsightly boxes until he paused and raised a lid. There in a winding sheet lay the earthly remains of Loo Foo, a laundry-man who had worked for Gee Wah at No. 170 Third avenue.

The wan face, the skin tightly drawn over the prominent cheek-bones, which were thus thrown into bolder relief, and the sunken almond-shaped eyes, gave the corpse the appearance of having starved or gradually wasted away. Without going into particulars I learned from the physician in charge of the ward in Bellevue Hospital, in which he had died, that the cause of death was undoubtedly phthisis, the fatal enemy of the Chinese in America, but that he had, from the testimony of his friends, smoked opium to excess—an excess even for a Chinaman.

I regarded the features of the defunct slave to an unconquerable tyrannical vice in silence. The keeper had left me alone in the dead-house, and gone to his monotonous routine of every-day duties. Glancing up from amidst the crumbling mortal clay through the small window in the end of the building I saw, amid the panorama of moving craft of all descriptions on the river, a British merchantman. The sight of the Union-Jack brought back a train of ideas, not original, but none the less forcible in my mental formulation of them. I thought of the Anglo-Saxon, under the pretence of legitimate commerce, and the powerful protection of that flag, filching the poppy product from his tributary Indian Empire and forcing it at the bayonet's point on the people of China, there to be opposed only by the weak protestations of the higher classes, and readily received as a solace by the lower and more ignorant. Thus it was that opium smoking became a national vice, inseparable in its associations, so that the mere mention of either the habit or the country immediately suggests the other. Then the coolies, impelled by the monopolistic Six Companies, to whom they were mortgaged, if not actually enslaved, began their exodus, and soon the Pacific slope of our country swarmed with the low-priced laborers who imported the habit.

In 1868 the Anglo-Saxon in America crossed the Rubicon into the smoker's Elysium, and consequent Hades; and now China is forcing on the child country the slow but fatal dose which the mother country forced on her, and ten-thousand people have already taken the cup which must be drained to the bitter dregs.   In re-turn— it is always the poor and the weak who must suffer—the climate kills the coolie.

I saw in all this, if not practical retribution, at least a poetic justice.

"What will we Americans do about it?"

FINIS.

Milton Keynes UK
Ingram Content Group UK Ltd.
UKHW042310160224
437951UK00004B/358